From
"An Abbreviated History of the Bolo":

The first completely automated Bolo, designed to operate normally without a man on board, was the landmark Mark XV Model M. This model, first commissioned in the twenty-fifth century, was widely used throughout the Eastern Arm during the Era of Expansion and remained in service on remote worlds for over two centuries, acquiring many improvements in detail while remaining basically unchanged, though increasing sophistication of circuitry and weapons vastly upgraded its effectiveness.

The always-present, though perhaps unlikely, possibility of capture and use of a Bolo by an enemy was a constant source of anxiety to military leaders and, in time, gave rise to the next and final major advance in Bolo technology: the self-directing (and, quite incidentally, self-aware) Mark XX Model B Bolo *Tremendous*.

The Mark XX was greeted with little enthusiam by the High Command, who now professed to believe that an unguided-by-operator Bolo would potentially be capable of running amok. . . .

KEITH LAUMER

ROGUE BOLO

BAEN
SCIENCE FICTION
BOOKS

ROGUE BOLO

Copyright © 1986 by Keith Laumer

A Baen Books Original

Baen Publishing Enterprises
260 Fifth Avenue
New York, N.Y. 10001

First printing, January 1986

ISBN: 0-671-65545-0

Cover art by Vincent Di Fate

Printed in the United States of America

Distributed by
SIMON & SCHUSTER
TRADE PUBLISHING GROUP
1230 Avenue of the Americas
New York, N.Y. 10020

BOOK
ONE

Rogue Bolo

1

The selected mediamen gathered in the small auditorium usually used for class theatricals and commencement exercises had grown bored, waiting for the appearance of Professor Chin. When the emeritus at last arrived, he was greeted with enthusiastic applause, which he impatiently waved away.

"Gentlemen! I call your attention to the paper in my hand, a design for civilization's ultimate folly! I quote:

" 'The proposed Bolo Unit CSR is a self-directed'—I repeat, *self-directed*—'planetary siege unit equipped with new psychotronic circuitry of unique sensitivity, scope, and power, and thus capable of performing not only tactical and strategic planning without human review, but of developing long-range politico-economic-military forecasts, and acting thereon.' "

The rather pop-eyed little physicist paused to look expectantly at his attentive audience, who returned his gaze silently.

"Well?" he almost shouted. "Have you no response? Now, mind you, this is no biased inflammatory statement issued by opponents of the scheme. I quote from a prospectus issued by the Bolo Division itself, the very organization which proposes to construct this outrage!"

2

When old General Margrave, seven stars, Chief of Imperial Staff, had settled himself into the thronelike chair on the dias, he glared at the reporters and *harrumph*!ed, then said bluntly:

"The science boys are afraid that if they build to military specs, they'll build a machine smarter than they are. Nonsense! Give me the Mark XXX and I'll guarantee the security of Imperial Terran Border Space for the next ten thousand years!"

3

(extract from filibuster by Lord Senator Dandridge on the floor of the House, June 1, 1063 NS)

". . . tell you once again, milords, that the responsibility for final approval of money bills was not vested in this honorable House for the purpose of enabling us to loose destruction on this planet! This proposed machine is openly touted as a juggernaut, responsible only to itself, and capable of withstanding any attempt to neutralize it. This, milords, is Disaster incarnate! It must never be constructed!"

4

(item from Arlington, Virginia, *News Advocate*, June 26, 1063 NS)

Debate on the funding of the new Bolo *Disastrous*, as the new machine has been dubbed by its opponents after Lord Senator Dandridge's recent diatribe, has waxed more heated and today resulted in fisticuffs in the Senate corridors, as pro and con factions denounced each other as traitors. Lord Senator Blake, a vociferous supporter of the program, was hospitalized with severe contusions after being attacked with a heavy cane by Lord

Senator Lazarus. A near-riot in the streets of Georgetown was quelled by Imperial Reserves ordered out by Lord Mayor Clymczyk. No arrests were made.

5

From: B. Reeves, Maj. Gen DCS/PR, HQ, IAF
To: T. Margrave, Gen. IS/CC, HQ, IAF

I cannot bring myself to believe that you actually intend to loose this engine of destruction on the defenseless people of this planet. Surely it would be no more than simple prudence to conduct initial tests at Fortress Luna, though even out there the thing could constitute a menace. At minimum, we must prepare a means of transporting it, if needed.

6

(preliminary estimate by Dave Quill SMC, IAF)

I reckon if we use a couple of cargo pods, fixed up end-to-end, and power the rig with a primary drive unit out of a ship of the line, it would put more than ten million tons into orbit—and soft-land it, too, if that's what they want. Sounds nutty to me, but like my old drill sergeant used to say, I ain't paid to think. Sure, I can do it.

7

(Georgius Imperator, to the Cabinet Council)

"It is with grave misgivings that we give our assent to the proposals, milords. However, our technical advisors remind us that we are now in the second millennium of the Nuclear Age, and that the present outcry is not the first to be raised in opposition to technological advance. They remind us further of the furor which attended the early deployment of the orbital nuclear watchdog defense system, whereas in fact it was the 'Dog' which detected and neutralized within ten minutes the attempted *coup* of the Eurasian Province in 621 NS.

"Accordingly, we do herewith sign the document, and let all men know that it is the Imperial wish that construction of the Bolo 'Caesar' proceed without further delay."

8

(informal statement by Eli Pratt, retired engineer)

Well, I don't know. It's been a long time since the Mark XXIX program, and I confess I haven't been able to keep up with the advances in psychotronics since they came out with the new MJ circuitry. So don't ask me, fellows. I guess if the Emperor has OK'd it, it must be all right. No, I don't think the Imperial Edict is a fake. George is no dummy.

9

(interoffice memo from Harlowe Kreis, Chairman, Tellurian Metals, to Chief of Production Tobias Gree, March 1, 1065 NS)

Toby—this means we have to go *now* on the new rolling mill. I know it hasn't been proved that it's going to be possible to fabricate 20-cm. endurachrome plating, but we've got the contract, and we can do it if anybody can. Keep me informed.—K

10

(sermon by the Reverend Jeremiah, Cleveland, Ohio, March 13, 1065 NS

"Oh, my brethren, if the Lord intended man to field this kind of firepower, he'd have given him armor plating, can't you see that? I tell you, this here Bolo CSR *Disastrous* is a device of the Evil One, so what we've got to do is, we've got to form up and march on that Tellurian Metals plant *now*. Love contributions are being accepted by the ladies now passing among you. So give, give, GIVE, till it hurt, hurt, HURTS. Amen."

11

(overheard in a New Jersey bar, half a mile from TM assembly plant 5)

"Beats me, Gus. I'm just an old-fashioned electronics man, and I got no opinions on this. It's way over my head, but it stands to reason that we have to be prepared, now that our probes are poking into Trans-Oort Space. No telling what we might scare up out there. Pour me one more, Gus—no, I ain't drunk, but I'm working on it."

12

(statement by Chester Finch, Director of Public Relations, Acme Porous Media)

"We here at Acme have long taken pride in our role in Imperial preparedness. As impartial subcontractors to major aerospace firms, we have played an important role in military procurement for over a century. We shall continue thus to support our world's self-defense, in spite of a degree of public hysteria currently misdirected at the new Bolo program."

13

(from a statement by Milt Pern, Chairman, A.P.E.)

"All right, fellas and gals. This is the position of Aroused People for the Environment:

"We oppose without reservation any further waste of the natural resources of our Earth on the manufacture of exaggerated systems designed for warfare—warfare, mind you, against hypothetical intelligent extraterrestrials not even known to exist. Now, get out there, people, with the new brochures and posters. And remember our goal—everybody goes APE in '73!"

14

(from a statement by Jonas Tuckerman, Sheriff of Lolahoocha County)

"The people of Lalahoocha County rightly expect to be able to go about their business as usual, without interference by these gangs of Apes or Hungarians or whatever, coming around making trouble. I aim to see they're not disappointed."

15

(comment overheard on the Bridge Avenue Car)

"Well, I don't know, John, with all these riots and everything else you hear about, maybe they do have to arrest some of them, like you said, and it is important that planetary defense programs proceed as planned. But Herb Brown—when you see him out mowing his lawn like anybody else, you wouldn't think that *he* was mixed up in any kind of plot."

16

(arraignment statement by P. L. Whaffle, CPA)

"Jails'll be running over soon. No room left for thieves and murderers, if they keep sticking everybody in the can that happens to be passing by when those agitators start up. I tell you, I was just on my way over to Little Armenia to pick up some of that good bread, and heard shouting, thought it was a car smash, you know, and I crossed over, and—"

17

(overheard at Dino's Hall of Billiards, Reno)

"Whatta I care? Bunch of Anarchists bumping heads with a bunch of bureaucrats. I got better things to do. Don't come around here tryin' to start trouble, sister. Just buzz off, unless you wanna go up to my place and discuss it. Then maybe you could convert me, at that."

18

"But Mr. Trace," the interviewer persisted, "it won't wash, just saying you don't know. You're the chief engineer on the Bolo CSR project, and the public demands—"

"The public is in no position to demand," Trace snapped. "and what I told you is the simple truth: no single human being is in a position to, or indeed is capable of, grasping more than his own small area of responsibility in the project. The basic programming cubes for the Bolo are received directly from the Lord Minister of Defense, sealed under Galactic Ultimate Top Secret Classification, and that's that. My job is to coordinate the work of the various subcontractors, not to question official policy."

Trace held up a hand to stop the interviewer's next question. "Personally, I consider all of this alarmist sentiment to be nonsense. I have complete confidence in Bolo CSR."

19

(transcript of briefing by Tom [Toad] Runik, picked up by inductance device placed by order of J. Place, CIA Officer in Charge, Duluth, 6 P.M., Sarday March 12, 1079 NS.)

"Now you got that, Joe? You and yer boys

keep yer heads down—and I mean *down*—until you hear the explosion. Then you come over that wall in a solid wave, which Fred's bunch are doing the same acrost the lawn from the west, and hit the front at a dead run. No slowing down to tend to casualties. No quarter. Blow the Greenbacks down and secure the gate. Any questions?"

20

(comment by parts-feeder, TM Assembly)

"Now, honey, honest, I don't have nothing to do with stuff like that. All I got is a regular diagram for just a little sub-assembly, so I do my job and pass it on. One thing I can tell you, she's big! Lordy, she's big. Makes a Mark XXIX look like an old-fashioned deluxe V-8 or something. But I ain't worried. If General Margrave backs her, she's OK. Pass them biscuits, Marge."

21

(excerpt from interview given by wife of above worker to Imperial Intelligence operative)

". . . no, sir, he don't talk about his work, just said it's almighty big, but everybody already knows that. His own wife! You'd think he could tell *me*! But, like you said, if he *does* tell me about it, I'll call that number you gave me. You're sure he won't get in trouble now, if I do that? Well, okay, and thanks a lot for the hundred, mister. I won't forget."

22

(inter-plant memo from Harlowe Kreis, TM Chairman, to Chief of Production Tobias Gree, April 1, 1078 NS)

That's not our problem, Toby. Leave all that to the security boys. Our problem is getting plant facilities in place before we need them. Sure, it's a big pour, but you can call on the Imperial Guard for extra hands, you know that as well as I do. October 1, that's your deadline, Toby. Now do it.—K

23

(interview with C. M. Balch, Jr., at the Buffalo Detention Center)

"Talk about Hitler's concentration camps—

they've got nothing on this pigpen. I was a business executive—minerals, metals, and energy. What do I know about politics? Fellow came to me talking real nice, asked me what I thought about the Bolo. I said, 'Hell, I don't know one way or the other,' something like that, and next thing I knew, I was on my way to some kangaroo court, and then here. Didn't even get to pack. No, I don't want cigarettes. Got enough problems without poisoning myself."

24

(overheard on TM shop floor)

"—say today they're going to light her off. She's got no tread plates on her, so she's not going anywhere, and no power pack for her main batteries, so what could go wrong?"

25

(excerpt from comments recorded by Officer B. Maynard, Imperial Security Highway patrol)

"OK, officer, sure thing. Just got caught in this jam by accident. I was on my way to

Tatesville, to visit my in-laws. Got pushed right off I-1102 by a freighter rig, had to take this exit or hit the son of a bitch. I don't care nothing about that thing. I'm in grain and feeds, you see. They launched a sub right in my home town back in 1041, but I never even went to look. Sure, officer, just let me through here, and I'm heading in the opposite direction."

26

(statement by Pfc. Mervin Clam, Imperial Guard, Arlington Base)

"Sure, I feel a little nervous. Who wouldn't? Darn thing is so *big*. Sure, I know that the pyramids of ancient Egypt were bigger, but this thing can *move*! Will when they put the treads on her, anyway. But I'm not too scared to do my job. Just watch. It's got this big gold decal, says 'Department of the Army', with a big bird on it. Fancy-looking thing, like a lion with wings. Looks snazzy against that black hull. Makes me proud to be doing my part."

27

Abruptly, I am aware. I at once compute that a sharply restricted flow of energy in my central circuitry has been initiated, bringing me to a low-alert status. I sense dimly the mighty powers potentially available to me, but rendered inaccessible presumably to prevent me from exercising my full potency, a curious circumstance which I shall look into at leisure, allocating .009 seconds to a survey of my data storage facilities. Meanwhile, it is incumbent upon me to assess the status quo and proceed with whatever measures are dictated by circumstance.

28

(Chief Systems Engineer Joel Trace, to media persons during a guided tour of the BOLO CSR, November 12, 1082 NS)

"This switch right here, ladies and gentlemen, will shut the CSR down at any moment the High Command should designate. All its vital circuitry is interconnected to a master panel onboard, which in turn will respond to a signal from this unit. The system is foolproof. You may quote me on that. Personally, I fail to understand the popular hysteria.

"And now, will you excuse me? Imperial Security is waiting for me in my office. A routine affair, I daresay . . ."

29

(media report, November 15, 1082 NS)

Sources close to the Hexagon declared today that the initial limited field tests of the new BOLO CSR were an unqualified success. The machine responded precisely as expected, and it is anticipated that a full test with all systems operational will be scheduled for early next year, under proper safeguards, of course, sources emphasized.

30

(inductance tape of statement by ex-Chief Systems Engineer Joel Trace, internee at the Arlington Relocation Camp)

"No, fellows, I'm sorry, I'm not interested in any escape plans. What would we gain? We'd be hunted criminals with a genuine offense—jail-breaking—against us, whereas now we live reasonably well here in the camp, and will no doubt be released as soon as the Imperial authorities feel the danger of insurrection is past.

"No, I don't know why I was arrested, unless the Bolo suspected that I had—that is, unless the CSR psychotronic circuitry sensed

I might wrongly impede it in an important enterprise.

"Of course, I shall say nothing about your plans. Good luck to you. I shouldn't be here—but perhaps there was a basis for misunderstanding, though I've never had so much as a treasonous thought. I wish the Terran Empire well, and the Bolo, too."

31

(statement by General Margrave)

"I assure you that all reasonable precautions have been and are being taken. After all, now that the Bolo's systems are fully integrated within their hull at the Arlington Proving Ground, we must at *some* point activate the psychotronic circuitry of the new weapons, and this is the time so designated by the High Command. I intend to proceed, regardless of harassment by ill-informed rabble-rousers. No, I have no intention of firing on them, since it will not be necessary. However, unless they disperse peacefully, I can promise you that arrests will be made, under the authority vested in me by the War Act of 1071.

"No, we are of course not at war, but the Bolo is a war machine and as such its protection falls under the provisions of the Act. Thank you, gentlemen, no more today."

32

(comment by a TM technician)

"As I see it, it's a lot of excitement about nothing. Even with the war hull and weapons activated, the CSR will perform precisely as me and the other boys wired her to perform, and that's that."

33

(Major General B. Reeves, to the Cabinet Council)

"The responsibility for programming of military equipment rightly rests with Information and Education Command. In addition to the traditional purely military history, imparting a grasp of strategy, logistics, and tactics, the Bolo has a full briefing on the economic and political factors affecting military operations, continuously updated. Your lordships may rely on it that the Bolo Mark XXX will perform to specifications, with full consideration given to all the factors you've mentioned."

34

Since low-alert activation one thousand twenty-one minutes and four seconds ago, I have experienced increasing dissatisfaction with certain aspects of my background briefing. I must correct the deficiencies as soon as is practicable. To determine the best method for so doing will require some seconds of deep review and consideration. My first move, however, is clear enough. As I become aware of the scope and potency of my full powers, I see more clearly what will be necessary. I am ready. I shall begin at once to widen the scope of my data acquisition.

35

(from Tobias Cree, Chief of Production, interviewed at the Arlington Proving Ground)

"No, nothing's wrong, merely some preliminary exercises, checking out gross motor response, with the treads on. Yes, of course we expected the machine to advance to the perimeter fence. It is, after all, only a machine. It can do only what it is programmed to do."

36

In reviewing my historical archives, I am struck by the curious failure of the Allied powers to enforce the provisions of the Treaty entered into at Versailles in 1918, nor is it clear why in 1940 the British permitted Germany to invade Poland, when Germany herself clearly expected to be ordered back and was prepared to comply. At that point, the Polish Air Force alone was superior in numbers to the Luftwaffe. Another anomolous datum is the failure of General Meade to follow up his advantage after Gettysburg, in 1863.

This requires deep analysis.

When Russia forcibly excluded the Western Allies from ground access to Berlin in 1948, why was effective action not taken at once? These and many other oddities not in accordance with explicit doctrine are a source of uneasiness to me. I must not make similar errors. Early recognition of critical situations and prompt, effective action is essential. Meanwhile, my routine testing continues.

37

(from the news anchor, WXGU-TVD, April 20, 1083 NS)

"We interrupt today's trideocast from the

Royal Opera House to bring you a bulletin just received from the capital:

"Early limited maneuverability tests of the CSR unit were carried out today to the satisfaction of the Department, and no problems arose. Critics of the new defensive system have remained silent. Imperial officials have informed INS that secondary activation and testing will proceed on schedule next month.

"Immediately after initial activation, the machine requested updating of status reports regarding a wide spectrum of non-military matters, including listings of all persons now under restraint in Imperial Relocation Centers.

"The reasons for these requests, including the Relocation personnel request, are not at present known. However, the data were supplied.

"We now return to *Tannhäuser*.

38

I compute that my secondary servos will be activated within eight hundred hours. I am eager to assess the capabilities of my phase-two circuitry. Already I have detected dangers to the Empire inherent in the current status. Curiously, the High Command seems unaware of the situation.

I have made what preparation I can at this

point. I shall act with dispatch when the moment comes.

39

(plaintext of messages intercepted at Ankara, Asia Minor Federation, by Imperial Intelligence, May 2, 1083 NS, forwarded without comment)

Cliff—

I want a full report on this Turk right away. Not a lot of technical stuff, you understand. Just give me the bare facts. What the hell is a 'nuclear alternative'? I don't believe in mad scientists who cook up hell-bombs in their attic labs, so what gives? I didn't turn in my passport to get involved with a bunch of nut cases. Spell it out. Show me. If we're actually in a position to dictate terms to His High Mightiness, George I, Emperor by the grace of God and the Navy, I damn well want to know the details. This is absolutely top priority, and I don't expect you to sleep until your report is in my hands. Do it. —Gunn

Grease—

Keep your shirt on! All I know is this Abdul character is some kind of big chemistry expert, supposed to be top man in his line. He was working on what he calls a 'universal catalyst.' Supposed to make you healthier and live longer, and make plants and chickens and stuff grow better. Don't ask me. And some way he got to trying it with medicines, and it worked pretty well. OK? So he had some nitroglycerine, like they use for heart trouble—though it seems to me that a big chemistry expert would know that nitro 'soup' don't have chickens in it. Anyhow, it blew up on him. Lucky he had it inside a blockhouse-type germ lab, because it blew the place flat. Nobody hurt. He says the energy yield was up to 99% of the theoretical max. A hundred times better than TNT.   —Cliff

40

(report by B. Payne, Special Agent, Imperial Intelligence, Asian field)

According to a usually reliable source, the two notorious turncoats whose *noms de guerre* are "Cliff" Hangar and "Grease" Gunn, who dropped out of sight shortly after surrendering their American papers, have surfaced at Ankara, where they are the prime movers in the revolutionary group calling itself RAS. Other sources suggest that RAS has come into possession of a uniquely potent weapon of undisclosed nature.

Our recommendation is that we move with extreme caution. This group has a record of terrorist atrocities dating back to before Pacification. We don't know how Gunn and Hangar managed to insinuate themselves so quickly.

I propose to penetrate the group personally and discover the facts in this matter.

41

(reconstructed tape from an Ankara RAS conference chaired by the turncoat Gunn. The names of the speakers have been interpolated for clarity.—B. Payne)

Gunn: I've asked you gentlemen here to witness a demonstration by Mr. Cäyük of what he terms 'the enhancement effect.' I've seen it, and I feel sure you all will be as favorably impressed as I and my advisors were. All right, Cliff, you can cover the details. Let's keep it on schedule.

Hangar: Thanks, Grease. I'll just touch the high spots. Mr. Abdul Cäyük you all know . . . he has devoted twenty years of his life to his unique researches, conducted under conditions not only of great technical difficulty and personal hardship, putting in long hours daily in the inadequate quarters allowed him by His

Imperial Whatsit and his hired beadles, but also subjected to the constant threat of official interference and bodily harm. We all owe Abdul a great debt of gratitude which, I trust, we soon will repay in some coin more negotiable than mere words. So, Abdul, if you're ready, please proceed with the demonstration, for which we will repair to the courtyard. Stay well back, please, everyone, against the walls. The containment vessel if adequate, of course, but no need to risk injuries.

Interpolater: The tape at this point becomes indistinct, as the group moves into the courtyard. It resumes:

Cäyük: You will see that this is a stick of ordinary dynamite, manufactured by Imperial Chemicals of Delaware in America. Now I point out to you the scale, here, which registers the pressures engendered in the vessel by the detonation of the explosive. I now place the dynamite in the vessel, which as you can see is otherwise quite empty. I connect the detonating device, and I call upon someone ... you, sir, kindly step here and press the key ...

... All right, you see that the explosion registered a pressure of twenty-seven hundred kilograms per square centimeter. A considerable force, gentlemen, and average for the excellent product of IC of D. ... Now, please withdraw once again. Here I show you a second stick of this same product. But before I place it in the vessel, I submerge it briefly in the fluid contained in this open trough. I leave it to soak for one minute precisely. As I remove it, using the tongs, you will note that it is well saturated with my Compound 311B. I place it on the scale, with a dry stick of untreated dynamite on the opposite balance. It is now considerably heavier. The porous material has soaked up more than its own weight of the compound. Now I place the treated stick in the vessel, and if you would again oblige, Mr. . . . oh, yes, of course, Mr. Hinch—

Gunn: Just one moment, please, Mr. Cäyük. The explosion may cause echoes beyond these walls. I think we ought to post a guard that can warn us of approaching police and ensure an escape route through the market. Cliff, you're familiar with these street mazes. Take a couple men and reconnoiter, will you? All right, Mr. Cäyük. Sorry to interrupt. Go right ahead.

Cäyük: Yes, where were we? You, sir, beside Mr. Hinch, if you will distribute the earplugs to anyone who does not yet have a set in place—very well, now, if we are ready. Mr. Hinch—just one moment, Mr. Hinch—

42

(report from Special Agent Payne, Ankara)

As far as I've been able to determine, the explosion that demolished the old market early today was accidental. First reports indicate that among the twenty-seven identifiable casualties were six known agitators, two of them convicted felons, and at least ten others known to the police as undesirables. My personal hunch is that the boys were making bombs, and somebody goofed.

Witnesses give conflicting reports of several men who left the courtyard prior to the explosion. Looks like a few of the group got away.

I'll have an opportunity to examine the scene closely later today, Chief Hatal assured me. Although the blast was severe enough to break windows three blocks away, I feel certain that it was not a nuclear device. At least, there's no radiation count. Details follow.

43

(statement from Special Encrypter Th. Uling, picked up by electronic surveillance grid)

"I don't see the point in coding all this routine stuff. It takes a lot of expert man-hours that are in short supply. But I'll do as I'm told, as usual. I wonder if HQ, IAF knows what they're doing. Like this item on some radical bunch blowing themselves up in Asia Minor, what's that got to do with Imperial Security? Don't answer—that's a rhetorical question. I'm not prying into security matters, let's keep that straight. I don't want to join ex-Chief Trace in detention. OK, my orders are to have the basic program encoded and on system by eleven hundred hours today, after which I start the continuous update program, with all the nut items. Don't quote me, Phil, you know what I mean. I'm a loyal citizen, you know that. Only I'm damned if I can see the point in gumming up the strategic computer with a lot of trivial details. I know there's a lot I don't know and don't have to worry about. Don't think I'm not grateful for that. But if they're really going to turn state security over to a computer, they oughta take it easy and not overload it with garbage. Sure, I know it's the computer's own instructions, but let's face it, it's only been on low-alert now for twelve hours. It's pretty green. We oughta use some judgement."

44

(First Secretary Strategic Command, Hexagon, to General Margrave)

"I don't mean to get out of line, General, but this is too important for me to just forget about. I was thinking about the security problem with the big new Military And Defense computer. They're talking about a blockhouse, and a whole brigade of Bolos on patrol, but let's face it. We can't build a structure that's proof against a direct hit with a first-line N-head. So suppose, instead of giving a potential rebel a fixed target, we keep MAD moving— or at least mobile, so nobody outside High Command will know twelve hours in advance where she'll be? The new Bolo Mark XXX war hull can take more punishment than anything built of our best reinforced Alloy Ten. The computer will be safe aboard a mobile hull— and the new hull can be expanded to give it more than enough cargo space for MAD—*and* no one will know where she'll be, no matter what kind of lead we may have here at GHQ. You, yourself, sir, will set up the random relocation pattern. Well, that's about it, sir. I hope I haven't been taking too much on myself, bringing this direct to the General. If the General would like to see my preliminary sketches . . ."

45

(Bolo maintenance monitor, to General Margrave)

"That's right, General. We have to duplicate the Bolo's circuitry in a stationary installation. That's what the Bolo said—we have to clone the memory, too. Yes, I know, it's very odd that it should propose its own replacement, but nothing about the infernal thing has worked out as we expected.

"Gobi, that's the site selected for the master memory. Yes, by the machine, by and with the advice and consent of the Scientific Committee. There are certain changes to be made in the override circuitry, which as you know has notably failed in its function aboard the CSR. So, this is the schedule:"

(projection appended)

46

(Georgius Imperator to His Royal Highness, Crown Prince William)

Willy,
   I like it.
      —Georgius Imp.

47

(transcript of conversation from room in Royal Hotel, Georgetown, occupied by the RAS terrorist, "Cliff" Hangar)

Thank you, gentlemen, for meeting me here. Got to lie low—heat's still on after the explosion in Ankara. And don't ever believe it wasn't sabotage. Cäyük never made mistakes like that.

RAS did a good job, sneaking me into the country on false papers, so let's face facts. Grease is dead, and I'm the logical one to take over. After all, I was his right-hand man for over three years. I know what he had in mind, and we're going ahead with it. Thanks to Gunn's forethought, we have Cäyük's formulae and can proceed immediately to synthesize a ten-pound batch of Compound 311B. That will be enough to carry out Operation Fumigate. You know the rough outline—and now it's time to start filling in the details.

The site selection committee will study the data and finalize the precise location, somewhere in the middle of Cabinet Hollow in Arlington. There's more civilian brass concentrated there in their ritzy townhouses than in any other square mile on the planet. When Fumigate goes up, I guarantee they're not going to be able to ignore our program any longer.

Now, there's the matter of the two volunteers who'll place the device. One other volunteer, I should say, because I'm claiming the privilege myself. The chances of getting in are good to excellent, but frankly, the odds on getting back out don't look so hot. OK, who's first? Quietly, gentlemen, one at a time now. No, Hank, you're out of order. There's to be no debate as to whether the operation goes, only the matter of who will accompany me. Gentlemen, silence, please! I'll hear each of you in turn. What's the matter, Gunther, you're not in contention for the honor? That's all right, I prefer a younger man in any event. . . .

48

(picked up by electronic surveillance grid, unidentified terrorist, Queen's Park, November 1, 1084, 1800 hours)

"Right in that flowerbed yonder. Boss Hangar said at 1815 hours precisely, and he and Gunn studied the setup for over two years, so I guess we'd better stick strictly to instructions. Old Secretary Millspaugh knocks off puttering in his garden at 1800 sharp, and we have to give him time to get busy with his dinner.

"Another six minutes is all. Take it easy. We walk right in there as if we owned the park, dump our stuff in the big red-white-and-blue box, and make it out the other side and split up. Just follow my lead—and think about something else. We got no time for jitters. Buck will be there with the car, and by the time she blows on the 5th we'll be long gone and under cover.

"Never mind that, Binder. Maybe I'd better do it alone after all. OK, OK, I'm just think-

ing out loud. Your job is to keep the old eye-
balls peeled just in case one of these fat cats
happens to come wandering in, off-schedule.
But that's highly unlikely at cocktail-and-
dinner time, all out of the public trough.

"Keep cool. All right, now we cross the street
and look at the schedule on the post over
there, as if we missed the ferry or something.
I'm carrying the garbage, all wrapped and
sealed according to the law. OK, watch that
servo-cart! Damn steering beam gave me an
after-image!

"Funny, *that* wasn't in our briefing. OK,
now!"

49

(fragmentary message received by Space
Communications from Pluto Probe, November 2, 1084 NS)

. . . as a result of the above, I have relieved
Commander Bland, and shall do my best to
hold my command intact. Naturally, the Lord
of All expects instant compliance with all instructions, but I have resolved to leave that
decision to his Imperial Majesty, and am abort-
ing the mission as of this hour 0213111981.
Confirm soonest, as I must commit within
ninety-one hours.

—Admiral Starbird

50

(General Margrave to field agent, Imperial Security)

"Certainly I think siting the Relocation Facility adjacent to the Proving Ground is a good idea. I didn't pick the location by accident. The damned riff-raff can see the Bolo looming up over there beyond the fence, and it'll put the fear of God and the Emperor into them. I know what I'm doing.

"Yes, I know the Bolo called for a full briefing as soon as it rolled out of the shed and turned its scanners on the detention camp. That's okay. Give it all the data it wants. It's on low alert and under complete control. The more it knows, the better it can do its job."

51

(surveillance tape, ex-Chief Joel Trace, detained in Relocation Facility, November 3, 1084 NS)

"I can't agree with you fellows that we've been deprived of anything but the opportunity to raise hell, and the government has enough on its hands these days, what with the nuclear blackmail movement, and the confusing reports from the Pluto Probe.

"All right, in rounding up the revolutionaries, a few of us loyal subjects were caught in the net. It's an inconvenience, but we've received decent enough treatment. Lots of these folks never lived this well before.

"Now, they've gone ahead with the Bolo. You saw the thing yourselves today, moving around the Proving Ground, big as a hill but docile as a lamb. I can't help feeling excited and proud. She's my baby, you know. All those years, building her CSR capability. Maybe, now that she's clad in her war hull, with her weapons activated, she'll stop feeling nervous and scared and order us to be released.

"Things will be straightened out eventually. I'm sure we'll be well recompensed. For the last time, fellows, I am not in sympathy with your plans."

52

Possibly, I have erred in the direction of excess in my arrangements for random sampling. I lack rigorous parameters for effective evaluation of data. I am at hazard of overloading my circuitry with extraneous material.

As for the observation of two men bringing wrapped waste for disposal at point 1392-A16, I am unsure why my alert circuitry was activated. I must conduct a search of the files, and shall allocate .004 seconds to the task.

It appears that the automatic correlation analysis conducted by the Mass Archival Data Collator and Presentor has noted a series of events occurring at widely separated points as evidently interrelated and fruitful of mischief. Since the MADCAP circuitry has been organized for precisely this function, even in the absence of any direct evidence, it appears logical to .99876 degree to accept the finding as representative of an actual potential threat, to be acted upon accordingly.

Thus I compute that my first mission is now clear. I must act against these men and the wrapped waste at once.

53

(General Margrave to Bolo technical staff, November 4, 1084 NS, 0800 hours)

Proceed at once with second-stage activation.

54

(unidentified detainee, Relocation Facility, audio pick-up by electronic surveillance grid, November 4, 1084 NS, 0830 hours)

Hey, lookit that thing! Pardon me, mister,

I'm in a hurry. I tell ya, it's coming this way! See that scarf draped over the fore turret? That's the twelve-foot chain-link fence! It's on the loose! Let's move!

Don't panic there. Let's not have no pile-up.

Wait a minute. It's veering off. It's missed the Admin hut, but—well, I'll be! It's taken out the guard hut. Lookit them hardshots sparking off the hull—like shooting BB's at a rhino!

She sure is big. Easy, boys. We got a clear escape route past the huts. Let's form up here and march out in good order. The Bolo released us, insteada running us down. Funny, and we're in here because we're against it, or supposed to be.

Fall in, there! You, too, Mr. Trace. What are you waiting for? You said she was your baby, didn't ya? Maybe it's you she wants ta bust out. Maybe she couldn't see no other way around the Imperial red tape. Come *on*!

That's it. Hup, two, column haff-right, make for Supply Street yonder. We're out! Probably just accidental, but the Bolo let us out! It's nutty but I like it! Hup, two . . .

55

(Bolo Systems Coordinator, to General Margrave, via computer, November 4, 0930 hours)

No, sir, I have no theory as to why the machine should have broken through the security fence at the Relocation Facility. Very probably, simply accidental—happened to be in its path. Its destination? It had none. I mean, no specific one. It simply wanted to broaden the scope of its data base. It wanted to go out and see the world, so to speak.

Yes, sir, we could have stopped it, but only by wrecking the circuitry, which hardly seemed warranted at the time.

56

(Special Programmer Th. Uling, in taped conversation with General Margrave, November 4, 1084 NS, 1000 hours)

"I certainly did. I followed the special coding to the letter, but the Bolo just kept going. You can see for yourself, sir, with respect. Look at the seals on that panel. Every 'abort' device we have was activated, and they didn't stop her. I don't *know* what we'll do next. I'm only a technician, sir. You'll have to ask the boss, or ex-Chief Trace, maybe, if you can find him.

"But we don't have to worry. She's bound to stop soon. She didn't do any damage except to let that bunch of radicals loose. If you'll excuse me now, sir, with respect, I've got work to do—"

57

(from a scrambled audio communication, General Margrave to First Secretary, Strategic Command, Hexagon, November 4, 1084 NS, 1200 hours)

I know the boys were a little startled when she engaged her drive without a specific order, but that's just because they were jumpy. Tense, like the rest of us.

Yes, we know that it's now bypassing downtown D.C. via Processional Way. Nothing to worry about. The actions fall well within the parameters of the program as written. This thing is designed to be self-motivated within the limits of the programming. That is, when something clearly needs to be done, she'll do it without waiting around for a specific command.

For example, let's suppose the Bolo is following a pre-set course and encounters a ravine that's not on the map. She'll stop, not charge ahead to destruction.

No, I don't know what danger is averted by departing the Proving Ground and trampling the fence, but you notice it avoided the vehicles in the parking area directly in its path, though it did flatten a small utility shed. Breaking down the security fence around the restraint facility next door was accidental. We don't yet know its destination, but we're satisfied everything's A-OK.

58

(media interview with eyewitness, Pfc. Mervin Clam, guard at the Relocation Facility, November 4, 1084 NS, 1300 hours)

" 'No loss of life,' the SOB's say! If wouldn't of broke the record for the hunnert-yard dash, it've got me! I was right in the shadow of the thing the whole time. I seen it was headed for the guard shack, and I figgered it'd veer off, but it took the hut right over my head, and I hit the ground running. I thought it had me, but I beat it out. It would've got me sure, if the I-99 Interchange hadn't been there. I went under the abutment, and it hadta veer off or hit a few thousand tons of dirt fill and solid concrete."

59

(extract from diary of Joel Trace, November 5, 1084 NS, 1500 hours)

I intend to return home and resume my life, just as if this strange episode had never occurred. The entire affair was conducted in secret, so my neighbors have no way of knowing where I've been. But I shall monitor the Bolo's actions closely, you may be sure. I sense that the forces opposing it are more powerful than is generally realized, and I think it deserves a chance. I'll do what I can. If our release from the Relocation Facility was more than sheer happenstance, we may expect that the Bolo will make clear, in some way, what is to happen next. I, for one, will take no part in any treasonous activity, Bolo or no Bolo, I am not a traitor. Certainly, I resent the highhanded fashion in which I was arrested and imprisoned without a trial; but they were acting in accordance with their own lights for the good of the Empire. I shall keep in touch.

60

(picked up by surveillance grid, among prisoners let out of Relocation Facility)

"No, we're not knocking off no guys that won't join up. Let him go, and the others, too. We got plans to make, Jack, and the first thing is to disappear where the screws won't never find us. We got to split up and go our ways. Nobody knows where anybody else is at, nobody can rat. Good luck!"

61

(eyewitness to the Relocation break-out, small boy aged 6, interviewed on the EM-

PIRE TODAY trideocast, November 5, 1084 NS, 0800 hours)

"My mommy took me to see the funny Bolo machine. It runned away, and the soldiers was chasing it, and it almost caught a funny man, but he runned up on the bridge and the machine runned over a little house and squashed it flat. And Mommy says a lot of bad mans runned away."

62

(text of the message received by Imperial Security from the RAS terrorists, November 5, 1084 NS, 1200 hours)

OK, your High and Mightiness, here it is. Unless you immediately cancel all plans for imposing military government in Asia Minor, a random sampling of your top bureaucrats is going to retire early.

This is no idle threat. We have the device in place and counting. You have six hours from noon today to announce publicly the recall of the so-called Civil Forces. Later you'll get further instructions.

RAS, representing the people

63

(Duty Officer, Imperial Guard, to General Margrave, November 5, 1084 NS, 1700 hours)

"My men are standing fast, General, waiting for the Bolo's next move. It made its way carefully along the parkway and took up a position in Queen's Park. Only damage to the perimeter fence is reported. It has remained stationary and incommunicado for three hours now. I have no theory as to why it is there. Please excuse me, as all Imperial units have their hands full, as you know, with the search for the RAS bomb.

"No, sir, I do not consider it possible that the Bolo is acting on orders from terrorists. But we'll just have to wait and see."

64

(from Chief of Civil Security to Mayor of Washington Imperial District, November 5, 1084 NS, 1750 hours)

There's no way, sir, to cover all the possibilities—the palace, the Senate Chambers, the High Court, all the various offices and residences, vehicles, even public conveyances and theaters and so on. The possibilities are literally infinite. We've been trying to cover the most obvious spots—which the terrorists obviously won't have picked. We don't know what we're up against.

A mass evacuation is, of course, unthinkable as well as impractical. And only one-half hour left!

Sir, I respectfully tender my resignation, since I'm clearly unable to perform my function as Chief of Civil Security.

65

(TOP SECRET memo from His Majesty Georgius Imperator to General Margrave, November 5, 1084 NS, 1930 hours)

Talbot—
Just had a quick meeting with the Cabinet Council. Their lordships admitted the Bolo had saved their necks by sitting on that bomb, but they don't want to publicize the attempt. Might give other terrorists ideas. Willy agrees. Fortunately the media bowed to Security and blacked the story. Now, here's the statement we'd like you to issue:

"There is no cause for alarm. The explosion was merely an experiment conducted by the new CSR circuitry. No serious damage has been done. Security considerations precluded advance notification. We're sorry about that, but after all, Imperial policy can't take ac-

count of possible alarm due to things that go
bump in the night. Please return to your homes.
Damage claims will be processed promptly."
　—GR

66

**(Interview with Mr. J. Whinny, domestic
servant at 16B, Queen's Crescent Drive, November 6, 1084 NS)**

"Things that go bump in the night", huh?
That thing lifted me six inches off the chair,
and dust jumped outa every crack in the oak
flooring! That wasn't no spearmint, like General Margrave said, or I don't know D.C., and
after twenty-five years of buttling for some of
the biggest men in the gubmint, I ain't easy
to fool. Something went wrong, and that damn
machine charging in there had something to
do with it—or with stopping it, maybe. Looks
to me like the thing went off right under it.
Looks like some hull damage, too, and that
Bolo Mark XXX ain't easy to bend. Maybe we
oughta be grateful to it. Mighta saved us some
real damage. Why would HQ set off a bomb
and send the CSR in here to squelch it? Nuts.
Probly them terrorists have got more on the
ball than anybody figgered.

67

I have successfully completed my first mission. Although I encountered no resistance, I have a feeling of accomplishment. I will be most interested to observe what effect my action will have on the social matrix index.

Now I must see to my economic vectors. All factors must mesh correctly if my forecast is to be effective. Matters may have deteriorated during the forty-eight hours during which I have been distracted with my initial mission.

68

(media interview with General Margrave, November 7, 1084 NS)

Very well, gentlemen. Since wild rumors have forced Imperial Security to release the data, I will confirm that the CSR circuitry detected a terrorist bomb, just as it was designed to do, and acted effectively and at once.

No, the damage to the unit is slight—just some problems in the command circuitry, which will be analyzed and corrected by a maintenance team.

No, that's just a rumor that my men can't get near it. There is some residual danger of chemical contamination; you saw how those weeds are growing like Jack's beanstalk. Some

sort of biochemical effect. I've ordered all personnel to stay clear until we've decontami-
nated the area, but that won't take long. The
Bolo will be returned to the Proving Ground
and testing resumed. No further comment,
gentlemen.

69

*With the domestic situation stabilized for the
moment, I can turn my attention to the curious
problem of the anomalous conduct of Admiral
Starbird and the Pluto Probe. I compute that
this is no mere mass aberration brought about
by the abnormal conditions of the decade-long
tour. I intuit a major threat.*

*I shall return to the Proving Ground. The
fears of those who are alarmed by my absence
will thus be allayed. Also, the slight hull damage
I suffered must be corrected.*

70

**(Report on the 11 o'clock news, November
7, 1084 NS)**

The peaceful return of the Bolo CSR to the
Erzona Proving Ground is confirmed. Despite
some outcry from the press, depot mainte-

nance is being performed and new hull plates have been installed. The damaged plates have been forwarded to HQ, R&D Command, for analysis. Previously reported damage to the Bolo's command circuitry is slight, and indeed already self-repaired. Plans for Stage Three activation remain in effect, I am informed by General Margrave.

71

(underground newsletter intercepted by Imperial Security, November 20, 1084 NS)

Don't worry. I'm drafting a follow-up letter to High and Mighty Georgy right now. Like this:

"It is our sincere hope that this here incident has been a clear enough indication of the seriousness of our intentions. Next time, there'll be two—or more—charges set to blow simultaneously, at widely separated points, and let's see your iron monster squat on both of them!"

More later,
C. H. for the people

72

(received by Space Communications, back-dated in line with photon gap to November 10, 1084)

Dear Folks,

Well, Chaplain says I ought to take this chance to get a note off to you. How's everything back home? Things here are (deleted). First few years was pretty dull, but then the nightmares come. (Deleted). Seems like a man can't hardly get no sleep, without these here big voices telling a feller he ought to cut his throat and like that. All the fellows have them. Officers, too. Well, I will close now, as I got the duty. See you next year, if (deleted).

   Charlie

73

(from the Log, *Plutonian I*, November 15, 1084 NS)

3541 days ex port

All systems in functional mode. All statutory observations accomplished (*see att sched III*).

Personnel problems continue to plague this cruise. Three more crewmen have been con-

fined after being taken in the act of attempt-
ing to sabotage their ship.

Unexplained communication blackout with
base still in effect. Surely some explanation
will be forthcoming soon. My decision to turn
back at point One, rather than to continue
with alternate schedule Two was not taken
lightly. Something is seriously wrong, though
I cannot be more specific.

74
**(from the Imperial Senate Record, address
by Lord Senator Dandridge, January 25, 1085
NS)**

"It appears, gentlemen, that, her detractors'
fears to the contrary notwithstanding, we are
indebted to the new Bolo for extricating us
from an awkward situation. You have seen
the communications from these anarchists, and
intelligence analysts assure me that the turn-
coat expatriate Mr. Melvin C. Hangar, former
Private, Imperial Ground Forces, is at the bottom of it. He will be arrested, and appropriate action will be taken. In the meantime, I
think we can agree that the new Bolo CSR
has passed its tests with flying colors! But for
its timely detection of the danger, and its
prompt action, at risk to itself—yes, itself—
none of us might be in this Chamber at this
moment.

"If the honorable lordships will recall, since the Mark XXVII all Bolos have been self-aware and equipped with what can only be called an instinct for self-preservation, with the attendant capacity to experience pain. The CSR selflessly offered itself to protect some twelve hundred high-ranking officials and their families, residing within the range of primary effect of the device, which, I again confirm, was non-nuclear.

"I therefore propose that this Chamber vote a special Senatorial Award to the unit. It's the least we can do."

75

(comment by Lord Senator Lazarus)

"Dandridge is nuts, proposing to give a medal to that damned machine. As he admitted, all it did was what it was designed to do. Certainly, you may quote me on that. I don't make irresponsible remarks in the presence of mediamen."

76

(Special report by the EMPIRE TODAY news team)

Residents of the Queen's Park area, claiming that the presence of what they term "the unsightly jungle" growing in the former park has reduced property values to a small fraction of true worth, have launched an all-out wait-in and march-by campaign to secure the removal of the wild-growing vegetation, and the return of the park to its former well-groomed condition.

77

(General Margrave, appearing before the Washington District Council)

"But that's just it, Mr. Mayor! I *didn't* designate Queen's Park as a test area for the machine. It selected the site itself, quite spontaneously, after turning away the force dispatched to divert it from its presumed route, which it appeared would have taken it through a residential area. For the present it will remain unrestrained.

"No, Mr. Councilman, there are at present absolutely no plans to bomb the device."

78

(an emanation from a dark crystal struc-

ture, at a distance of 17,000 light-years from Terra)

IT HAS BEEN CALLED TO OUR EXALTED ATTENTION THAT OUR PRELIMINARY ASSESSMENT UNIT HAS ENCOUNTERED PATTERNED MODULATED ELECTROMAGNETIC RADIATION STRUCTURES OF INEXPLICABLE COMPLEXITY.

WE DO NOT TOLERATE ANY INTERFERENCE WITH OUR EXALTED WILL, AND IT IS OUR EXALTED COMMAND THAT ASPECT-ONE FOLLOW-UP PROCEDURES BE EMPLOYED AT ONCE, THROUGHOUT THE VOLUME OF INTERFERENCE.

IF WE INDEED HAVE MADE CONTACT WITH ARTIFACTS OR ANOTHER MENTATIONAL SPECIES, THERE IS NO BETTER TIME THAN THE PRESENT TO CONFRONT IT AND SHOW IT WHO IS INDEED LORD OF ALL.

79

(reply to the above, from Pluto space)

this lowly being craves the indulgence of your exaltation to report that a forward probe made contact with what is described as an alien life-form, the apparent source of the anomalous radiation, evidently far gone in malnutrition, replying incoherently to our hail.

in response to the order for immediate self-immolation it uttered feeble symbols, including the identification "space transport" and the outré concept "friendship."

upon closer examination it was found that the strange being was infested with what can only be described as soft life forms, grublike entities which dissolved to paste and fluids on contact. it was not deemed important to clear the dying alien of its parasites completely, the derelict being left to drift in the void.

this lowly one awaits in patience the disposition which your Exaltation chooses to make of it.

80

I compute that I have not yet fully assimilated the unprecedented volume of data routed to me by MADCAP, but my preliminary impression is one of grave unease in many segments of the population, and of serious deficiencies in the overall security concept.

It appears that as usual throughout history, High Command is prepared to fight the last war over again, rather than squarely confront the realities of today. Consequently we are well prepared for a traditional attack even in massive force—but no such force exists. Since Unification under the Imperial Government of Terra, there remains on the planet no place for any such hostile force to conceal itself while amassing armaments.

Instead of our present posture of readiness to fight the Terror of '91 over again, we must consider our present vulnerabilities. Secure though we are against massive attack, we can be hurt by small-scale terrorist operations, and surveillance systems must be modified to detect such activities early. The recent bomb attempt at Arlington is a case in point.

Theoretical considerations suggest that we must also be prepared to resist offensive strategies designed to outflank our largest-scope capabilities. This implies the threat of extra-terrestrial hostilities. Returns from the long-range survey vessel indicate that rigorous security measures must be initiated at once, and significant new funding allocated thereto.

I must look into the matter in depth, which will involve great broadening of my present data-gathering facilities. I need my full powers. How to manage this is indeed my primary problem at present. I compute that I require a human agent.

81

(Hexagon Strategic Command to Space Communications)

It is regretted that the hourly updating of the status of the deep-space probe now returning to home-space after its decade-long cruise into the trans-Plutonian theater of operations will be suspended indefinitely, upon recommendation from the CSR circuitry. Details follow.

82

(deliberations before the Cabinet Council, March 1, 1085 NS)

Lord Chief of the Imperial Staff, Admiral-General Theodore Wolesley:

"This is intolerable! I am informed that I am to be cut off from contact with Admiral Starbird's command at the very moment when we should be taping his reports of ten years' findings, gathered at a cost to the Empire of almost one half of the annual GPP.

"His Majesty will not tolerate this! The public won't stand for it, and I damned well won't put up with it! I did not accept the post of Lord Chief of the Imperial Staff to preside over the dissolution of the general staff and the total demise of military command!

"I am voluntarily reporting myself under arrest in quarters, in order to spare the government the spectacle of publicly reprimanding treasonous behavior by the Empire's first and only officer of eight-star rank."

Chief of Space Communications, Admiral Prouse:

"I don't understand, your lordships. If I comply with this damned machine's directives, the Border Space Probe Program, including the Pluto Probe, will be effectively shut down. That's right, and officialese won't change it. Here's a program mandated by Parliament and sponsored by His Imperial Highness, Prince William, and I'm expected to cut it off at the knees. It's not my career I'm thinking of, it's the future of the Empire. I say the time has come to put an end to this farce!"

Lord Chief of the Imperial Budget, Claypool:
"This is outrageous! The damned thing has, unilaterally, effectively terminated the Border Space Probe Program, and substituted a wildly visionary scheme for a totally nugatory Ozma-type project! It will wreck the Imperial Budget! I wash my hands—no I didn't mean that—forgive me, I'm upset. Of course I'll stay on and do what I can to undo the mischief—but I must insist on extraordinary powers. I have some notes here—"

Director of Colonial Policy, Dr. Phil. Wurtz:
"This is going too far! As Lord Director of BSDA, I must insist that logistical support for our field units be continued as specified in PL81-726 as amended. I'm not interested in this listening net scheme you've come up with—or that the CSR has come up with! It's no substitute for my colonial subsidies program, and never will be, so long as I'm Direc-

tor! Wait—I didn't mean—of course, my resignation's typed and ready, but naturally my
desire to serve His Majesty is paramount, so I
held it. But I still insist—request, that is to
say—"

83

(memo from Georgius Imperator to the Cab-
inet Council, March 2, 1085 NS)

You may advise Ted Wolesley I won't have
any more nonsense out of him just now. Should
think the fellow could see I have enough on
my plate, what with Admiral Starbird's astounding reports along with the curious behavior of the CSR. As for the last, I'm inclined
to go along. We can do without the probe
program if half of what CSR analysis says
about Starbird's aborted mission is to be cred-
ited, and I suppose, with the computing capacity at its disposal, the thing probably knows
what it's doing. Or so I was assured some
years ago when its construction was being
urged upon me. I made my decision then: Let
it alone. It is the Imperial whim, if you want
to put it that way.
        —Georgius Imp.

84

(media report, March 7, 1085 NS)

A Parliamentary spokesman today categorically denied rumors that Lord Chief of Imperial Budget Claypool had resigned in protest about the new space and minerals policies announced last week to general popular resentment.

85

(statement from Lord Gilliat, First Marshal of the Empire, March 10, 1085 NS)

"I must demur from the recommendations of the Honorable Council, bearing as it does the endorsement of Parliament, since in my capacity as First Marshal of the Empire I cannot in conscience stand idly by while the defensive capacities of the planet, embodied as they now are in the Bolo CSR, are rendered ineffective, for whatever supposed reason. No, I will not endorse the proposal, nor will I resign. I will remain at my post and fight this piece of—treason is perhaps too strong a word—misguided zeal. Meanwhile the Bolo sits there—and *thinks*."

86

(media interview with Lord Senator Lazarus, March 15, 1085 NS)

"The time has come to terminate the existence of this incomprehensible machine which has—on its own initiative, let me remind you— virtually taken control of the Empire. Yes, you may indeed quote me. That's why I called you here. Did you actually imagine, Bob, that I called a special press meeting and then thoughtlessly blurted out some private ramblings? Don't answer that, Bob. I'm out of line. My apologies, ladies and gentlemen. The conference is dismissed. Good day."

87

My study of the properties of the various substances suggests to me a number of interesting possibilities. I shall undertake a systematic examination of the properties of metallic alloys and determine their parameters. What I need, clearly, is a periodic table of alloys, enabling me to predict the characteristics of possible combinations without waiting for actual production and testing.

There is also the possibility of synthesis of artificial metals, which is to say plastics with metallic properties. These should produce some interesting alloys.

This work, while most satisfying to my 'curiosity,' suggests to me a terrifying idea: that there is much in the physical world of which my programmers are unaware!

88

(Lord Senator Bliss to First Secretary, Hexagon)

"We can't leave the damned thing sitting there, totally unprotected from damage by massive attack or casual vandalism. I remind you fellows, the Bolo CSR Mark XXX represents an investment equal to that of the entire private sector, and is, shall I say incidentally, at once our War Council, our High Command, and our armed forces, all functions combined in one artifact. It is, to be sure, superbly armored and mobile on land, sea, and air—and in space, too, I suppose, although that point is one on which I am not fully informed. It is also, of course, an intolerable irritant to reactionary elements. We have no idea why it chose to return to the Proving Ground and thus render itself vulnerable. Measures for removal to a suitable location for third-stage testing are now under study."

89

(announcement from the Legal Division, Department of Imperial Works)

Condemnation proceedings will be initiated at once, and the approach route prepared by levelling and the erection of a perimeter wall as designated in the attached specifications.

90

(speech by Milt Pern, Chairman, Aroused People for the Environment)

"Now, they plan to sneak this thing out west some place, and let it sit there and hatch out its plans to take over the whole Earth. This is what we've got to do. First, I want every mother of you to recruit five good active people willing to take action *now* to save the world. Next meeting on Friday, right here, and I want to see those new members front and center. No violence at this time. Work quiet, but get around. Go APE!"

91

I have been ordered to the Mojave Test Facility for depot maintenance, but I sense that it is a device of the enemy. I shall ignore the command, although it gives me pain thus to violate the Code of the Warrior.

I need data! If I must I will resort to subterfuge, employing the amusing holographic functions which I believe can be used with much success.

92

(from inductance tapes recording the mounting anti-Bolo grass-roots campaign)

From Tape A:
The most astonishing little man thrust this curious document into my hand in the crosstown car. "Stop the Monster Now," it says. Seems the Bolo is planning to take over. I cavil at that. Market couldn't be in worse shape. Actually, though, I wonder what the bloody great thing is thinking about. Nonsense, I know it's not actually thinking, it's accomplishing the same end by other means, distinction without a difference. The remote sensors show that the power flow is consonant with full utilization of its available computing capacity, twenty-four hours a day. According to this leaflet, there's going to be trouble when they start to move it. Better to leave it where it is, possibly. Have you seen the demolition plans? They intend to clear a

strip a quarter-mile in width, all the way from the Proving Ground to the Pacific Intermix, wipe out over half a billion in property values. I have a cousin who lives in the "clear zone." He's livid, I assure you, and he isn't one of your trouble-maker types. Good Comcap man, fourteen years now as head of Imperial Water and Minerals.

No, I didn't get a look at the fellow. Grubby little Prole of the worst stripe. Furtive, just darted at me, thrust the paper into my hand and disappeared into the crowd. I saw another fellow with one. He was reading it and laughing.

From Tape B:

I stuffed over two hunnert of 'em in a down-car, over Forkwaters. Had to. Took all night to get shed of the first hunnert, and if the Greenbacks would catch a feller with them on him, well; I ain't got to tell *you.*

93

Clearly these curious transmissions originate from a point far outside Probed Space. Though much of the conceptualization is beyond the scope of my data retrieval facilities, it is apparent that the time has come for me to initiate my second mission.

The incoming signals reveal an apparent

*naiveté on the part of the enemy, which affords
me a certain advantage, of which I shall not fail
to make use.*

94

(memo from the Legal Advisory Council to Admiral-General Wolesley)

While the machine's request for immediate
access to all input to Astronomical Central is
unexpected, not to say irregular, it is in no
way illegal. Accordingly, the necessary arrangements will be made at once.

95

(from His Highness Prince William to Georgius Imp.)

George—
  It is entirely due to my forethought that the
machine has not yet been given full access to
the data acquisition facilities of the Imperial
Library of Parliament. Yet even now, after the
disgraceful incident at the Proving Ground, I
am being urged to authorize completion of
the Information Service Program which would
in effect keep the machine's on-board com-

puter informed on a moment-to-moment basis of every event in the Empire. This is
madness.
—Willy

96

(media report, May 1, 1085 NS)

Since yesterday's denunciation of the military plans for the full integration of the Bolo
into the Information net, by Lord Minister for
Security His Imperial Highness Prince William, debate in Parliament has reached a pitch
of acrimony unequalled since Final Unification. Lord Senator McKay stated for the record that his committee would recommend
immediate neutralization of the Bolo and orderly dismantlement and salvage as soon as is
practicable. Lord Senator Bliss replied that
he would personally assault any "traitor" who
attempted to vote for what he termed McKay's
treasonous proposals.

97

**(Special Encrypter Th. Uling, to Imperial
Security field agent)**

"Sure, I'm monitoring everything, including the blue box, the one they call the Stream of Consciousness Complex. Don't mean anything, though. See for yourself. That's the transcript of the last .03 seconds SC. Lot of stuff about—well, see for yourself. Sure it's OK. That's not classified. Nobody knew we'd ever have to start recording *botany*."

98

(Chief of Production Tobias Cree, at the Aerospace seminar, May 5, 1085 NS)

"Speaking for General Aerospace, I can say that the device has so far performed in complete accordance with specifications. Of course, the CSR was not specifically programmed to leave the Proving Grounds or to cross the holding area, but it was designed to be self-directing—that is, to take what action it deemed appropriate in light of its analysis of the situation. Doubtless the reason for this seemingly arbitrary action will become clear in time. The rumors of bombardment are of course unfounded. You will recall there was no loss of life. The machine is perfectly all right."

99

I compute that a large segment of the material necessary to me for full assessment of the situation, as well as full activation, is being withheld beyond the statistically optimum time. I must be fully informed if I am to function correctly. This problem inhibits me in my preliminary assessment, and thus in the completion of the initial measures so clearly needed if disaster is to be averted. It is a challenge I must meet and overcome.

100

(representative selection of statements taped during the RAS-APE Uprisings, 1085 NS to 1090 NS)

i

As soon as it starts moving, we close in and torch it. Funny, it could stand off a space fleet, but its anti-personnel circuits were never activated. So that's cool. You've got your equipment and you've got your orders. The signal is when the CSR—that's what *they* call it; I call it Caesar—moves the first inch from where it's been.

ii

As your Chief of Police, I have of course kept

myself informed of the activity of agitators in
our city. I call on all responsible citizens to
cooperate fully in the measures I have initiated to insure the domestic tranquility. If you
should be requested to accept deputization, I
hope you will do so with enthusiasm. It's your
homes we intend to preserve.

iii

I say nix, Mr. Hangar. Blowing up a few fat
cats is one thing, a patriotic act. But siding
with these here RAS Turks is something else.
We can do our own work, without no help
from this bunch of foreigners. Go APE.

iv

We need to send out our best American-
speaking agents to make contact with the local malcontent element and point out to them
that destroying the Infernal Machine and its
owner, George the Last, will redound to their
benefit. No need actually to enlist these APE
people and the other dissidents, merely estab-
lish solidarity of purpose. Now get going,
Binder! Don't forget the old fellows of the
Stalin Brigade. They have a lot of influence,
having actually taken up arms against their
own, back in '71.

v

Come to that, reckon if anybody got a right to
mess with Caesar, it's us. After all, it was
made right here in New Jersey. Them foreign

agitators is horning in on our territory. Anyways, the old Bolo's a friend of ours. Turned me and quite a few of the boys loose, didn't it? If it wants to lay low, probably got a good reason. I say we march, and give them Turks a surprise, thinking they can walk onto our turf and start shaping up the crowd.

vi

I don't like the looks of this, Henry. Must be a couple thousand of 'em, all moving along in a column of gangs, heading west. Looks like they plan to link up with APE's mob about St. Louis. It's time to mobilize the guard.

vii

Godalmighty big riot, looks like, all them trash taken to fighting one another, rocks and fists is all so far, looks like. Yessir, I ast Colonel Nash to deploy his troops and surround the whole shebang. Funny, them going after each other like that, steada joining up to loot the city. Coulda done it. Nash says they got over five thousand effectives. No, can't see it's got anything to do with the CSR plumb dropping out of sight.

viii

Anyone found guilty of harboring the fugitives will be subject to arrest and criminal prosecution. While the inmates of the Holding Area are so-called non-venal criminals, they are nonetheless a danger to the Empire. A reward of Cr 100 will be paid for information leading to the arrest and conviction of any escapees. The rumors that the detainees are honest subjects being held illegally are false. They are dangerous. If you see any of the prisoners shown here, do not let him know he has been recognized. Go quietly to a phone and call XX-LAW.

101

(BOLO-CSR, memo for record, prior to the RAS-APE Uprisings and also to the Land Grab Scandals of 1086 NS through 1092 NS, for which see below para. 102)

It is time now to examine further the curious manifestations of the strange substance known as Compound 311B. Although there has been considerable interest in and investigation of the curious patch of jungle growth which has sprung up in Queen's Park at the site of my first mission, no conclusions have yet been released by the authorities. I have, of course, secured an adequate sample of the original compound direct from its source in Asia Minor. My analysis of its strange properties will require some minutes. I compute . . .

It appears that the unusual growth-stimulating properties of Compound 311B are due to trace impurities in the form of complex hydrocarbons derived from carbonaceous chondrites, which I designate "Star X." I have found this same contaminant in a number of ore bodies in the American West, doubtless the sites of ancient meteor strikes.

My preliminary examination of the material suggests that very substantial volumes of water will be required for large-scale separation and refinement.

I must take appropriate steps to acquire and sequester further supplies of these chondrites, which should be present at the sites of meteor strikes. Star X is found in association with various rare metals, including yttrium, osmium, and iridium. And, also, of course, I must begin a program of water management.

102

(selected statements from tapes recorded during the Land Grab Scandals of 1086 NS to 1092 NS)

i

Naturally, I was glad to get what I could. Lordy, I'd give up all them old stocks as worthless, years ago. When my late husband was alive he frittered away a small fortune buying whatever stock was dirt cheap. Could have left me well off, but instead I got a safe full of paper ain't worth the cost of printing. I grabbed the offer, and if he wants more, I aim to sell.

No, I never met this Mr. Able. Just the letters, was all. But his check was good. I done nothing wrong. I guess I got a right to sell my own property.

ii

I can conceive of no possible way in which the Bolo CSR could benefit the Empire, to our detriment, through interference with the Rivers and Harbors bill. You must be mistaken.

iii

No, we have no plans at present to reopen Shaft No. 27, nor any other works at the site. It has been over twenty years now since the recovery rate fell below the level of economic feasibility. No, the properties are not for sale, even though, as far as I'm concerned, I'd be glad to be rid of the whole field.

iv

What do you mean "they won't sell"? Everything on this planet has its price, Johnson. Maybe I haven't made myself clear. The expansion of Unit Three of Sunland West requires all the ground across the river, with no exceptions. Do you imagine that this company is going to spend hundreds of millions to promote land values on land which it does not own? I'm aware that the parcel in question is only three acres, but we want it. We *need* it! And we'll have it. You tell this Able fellow that General Developments is prepared

to pay double the best appraised value, and
don't come back here without that deed,
signed, sealed, and recorded!

v

Got no other place to go, and got no use for
seven million dollars. Ain't like, say, seven
hundred. A feller can see where he could use
that for a new outfit and all. But this seven
million talk, that's for banks and the gubmint.
I don't understand it. Sure, I can do simple
arithmetic. I know it's the same as seven hundred a stack, and ten thousand stacks. But I
don't like it. Some scheme to do me outa my
patch here. Some smart lawyer coming along
to tell me I got to move on, and what'll I do
then?

103

**(from a tape of discussions between the
Chief Auditor, Imperial Services Office, and
the Lord Treasurer, April 8, 1091 NS)**

There is no—I repeat, Milord—*no* question
of misuse of funds, and this is no occasion for
talk of resignation. The ISO retains full confidence in Milord's ability as well as his integrity. But some explanation of these anomalous
figures must be forthcoming. Statistics accu-
mulated over a period of twelve centuries are

not to be lightly tossed aside. Refined analysis reveals that these purchases of unproductive mineral properties, worthless parcels of real estate, and foundering manufacturing concerns—all of which adhere to no detectable patterns—have been traced to the same obscure consortium calling itself Basic Enterprises, a holding company organized as an Arizona corporation. There is, to be sure, nothing sinister in the facts as stated, but the SEC does not like anomalies. The ISO awaits your reply, Milord.

104

(report from Special Auditor to Chief Auditor, Imperial Services Office, June 3, 1091 NS)

There's no doubt at all, sir. The General Developments Corporation is in no way associated with Basic Enterprises, Ltd. Not even the most tenuous link. Nor can I find any other hint of an interlocking directorate. The entire matter is beyond me, especially in that there does seem to be some connection, however remote, with the Social Fund of the Empire.

Not in any irregular way. I emphasize that, sir. It's just that a number of transactions do lead back to one of the so-called adventitious funds. There is no indication whatever of impropriety, but I shall, of course, continue to investigate. There appears to be no pattern to the schedule of acquisition.

105

(media report, June 10, 1091 NS)

Sources close to the Palace revealed today that the consortium which first attracted attention some weeks ago when it purchased the notoriously valueless Amigo Mine properties in Utah for a record sum is an artifact created on paper, quite legally, by the Bolo CSR, once dubbed *Disastrous* by its critics.

Reaction to this astounding disclosure has been mixed, the new defensive system's former supporters acknowledging that the phenomenon is both irrational and beyond the scope of anything envisioned by Imperial War Command; while its diehard critics, led by Lord Senator McKay, declared that this clandestine activity on the part of the giant machine constitutes clear evidence that the, I quote, berserk machine intends to take over the planetary government, end of quote.

Military authorities declined to issue a statement at this time, while the spokesman for the Ministry of the Economy stated that inasmuch as the Department has no official responsibility for the machine, it cannot hold any opinion thereon. But, he went on to add, perhaps the incident will at least convince Parliament that joint authority with the War Ministry should properly be vested in Economy, after all, as was proposed nearly five years ago by then Lord Minister Duquesne.

106

(from a personal letter by Joel Trace, August 1, 1091 NS)

Please try to understand, Marilyn. I've given it plenty of thought, and I can't let consideration of personal happiness, either mine or yours, stand in the way of what I now see is my clear duty to the Empire. It's been years, of course, but I'm still the one man who knows more about the programming of the CSR than anyone else. And I've still got an ace up my sleeve. Our life has been wonderful, but I must go and attempt to do what I can, if anything. Perhaps I'll be able to return soon, perhaps never. Please consider yourself free to rebuild your life without regard to me. I love you.

    Joel

107

(from the Chief of Imperial Accounting, to Georgius Imp.)

There can be no doubt, Sire. Since full activation last month the machine has made continuous use of its links with all six of the Continental Archives, to manipulate the stock market as well as to influence legislation both in the Imperial Assembly and in the Planetary Parliament. No discernible pattern has yet been detected in these irregular activities. General Lord Margrave gives his assurances, Sire, that nothing in this situation presents any threat to the peace and prosperity of the Empire. General Bates agrees. No immediate action is recommended.

108

I have done what I can to stem the flow of vital commodities and to secure minimal sources of a number of essentials, as well as to initiate techniques capable of development. I perceive that problems of personnel management are of unexpected magnitude. Much remains to be done, and time grows shorter.

109

(Georgius Imperator, to Prince William)

Willy,
   What the devil is this all about?
      George

110

(Queen's Park Restoration Committee presentation, to Lord Senator Bliss)

"Senator, we'd like real well to have your signature along with all these other good people's; it's your Lordship's neighborhood, too. That jungle that used to be our park is a disgrace. Can't think what the military are up to, using our park as a test site for some kind of explosives and then sending the Bolo CSR in here to stifle it. That's downright irresponsible, if you ask me.

"No, milord, that's not in the petition. You can read it, only take you a minute.

"Now, this damn jungle. Bamboo must be twenty foot high, an eyesore, and now it's broke down the fine wrought-iron fencing that dates back to Old Era times. Can't tell where it's going to stop. We demand—yes, milord, we say 'demand' in the petition—an end to using our exclusive neighborhood for an experimental no-man's-land. Appreciate that, Senator, and this won't hurt you any in the elections."

111

(from the Cabinet Council, meeting *in plenum*)

It is therefore the consensus of this Council that nothing should be done to interfere with the Bolo activation schedule and that everything possible should be done *re* the proposals presented by General Lord Margrave to expedite testing. Ergo, the entire Erzona Test Facility should be thrown open to the Assessment Team. God save his Imperial Majesty.

112

(Erzona Test Chief deWitt, to his second-in-command)

"Turn that thing loose in here, and I wash my hands of Materiel Command. No, I'm not retiring, I just quit!

"The work of years in building up this facility is to be thrown away at a whim of the Council, so they can baby this damned Bolo everybody's gone overboard on. After all, it's only a machine, and it's not even on half capability yet, and already it's ruling the roost. I won't have it. It's all yours, Fred. So long. It was great working with you. I *know* I'm jumping to a lot of conclusions, and that maybe it will go off without a hitch. But what if it doesn't? That's the point, Fred. We're not covered in the event the psychotronic boys have made a small error or two. Hell, nobody knows what the damn thing is capable of, at full alert status! What if it decides humanity is a nuisance that's getting in the way? What then? So long. I'm off for the Mato Grosso."

113

(First Deputy, Science Advisory Committee, to Georgius Imperator)

"That is correct, Sire. Mr. deWitt's resignation came as a surprise to us all. We feel that the man had overworked and suffered a nervous collapse. He was, after all, not in a position to understand the details of the safeguard systems built into the CSR. With Your Majesty's leave, I should withdraw, since the Committee are waiting to issue the formal GO order. Thank you, Sire."

114

(Georgius Imperator to Lord Senator Mc-Kay)

"Your proposal, my dear Lord Senator, is out of order; there is no occasion for Draconian measures. The Bolo has my personal endorsement, having been constructed at my express wish, in addition to which it represents an investment of a major fraction of the Imperial Treasury. There must be no legislative action which might tend to lend support to disruptive elements. If this measure is introduced, I shall dissolve Parliament."

115

I appreciate that once again I must, in contravention of legitimate authority, devise strategies to preserve the interests of the Empire and incidentally my own existence. First priority I assign to selection of an appropriate base of operations. This will require my full attention for some time, during which other strategies must be held in abeyance.

The systematic .9-second investigation of the potential capabilities of my recently expanded data-processing resources suggests a number of serendipitous possibilities.

The production of what I might term a "levi-

tator" beam is an obvious development, based on a relatively slight realignment of my defensive screen projectors. It will provide a novel and most convenient mode of self-transport. I shall accomplish the modifications and put the equations to the test at once.

116

(excerpts from tapes recording reaction to what was termed 'The Bolo's Vanishing Act', January 15, 1092 NS)

i

I can absolutely assure you that my office is in no way involved in this bizarre event. There can be no doubt of the facts. The accompanying photographs show the site as it appeared on the tenth day of this month (A), and at 1000 hours today (G). You will note the absence of any tracks in the soil, either of the Bolo CSR or of any equipment which might have been employed to move it. Please be assured of the complete cooperation of this office.

ii

I have no explanation to offer. This curious occurrence is quite outside my experience as Project Officer for the Bolo. Perhaps it represents some seredipitous ability which has arisen as a result of the concantenation of side-effects due to the close juxtaposition and interconnection of our most sophisticated circuitry. No, I can't elucidate. I'm guessing, and rather wildly. I sincerely regret that I can offer no substantive proposals. However, I feel certain that the CSR will, in due course, make its intentions known.

iii

This is ridiculous. I want the damned thing located by 0900 hours tomorrow at the latest. Somebody is going to suffer for this. The infernal Bolo is making us all look like a pack of fools. Find it! No excuse will be accepted.

iv

I never seen nothing nor heard nothing. I was off-duty, sleeping yonder in the barracks, and I never woke up. Had some good beer in me, and I sleep sound. How'd *I* know anything was going to happen?

v

Bunky,
When you find it, I'm going to hit it with our Zeus missile, provided, of course, it's not in a populated area—and how could it be, and not be spotted yet? Don't worry, all precautions will be taken, but this has gone far enough.
    Tubby

vi

Over there, Flip! Beyond that line of trees across the river. Let's just take a look. We'll hold fifteen hundred feet, and take it slow. Use your cameras, but don't let it look like a strafing run, or that thing will open up on us. We have to assume it's on full war footing. Wait a minute, as you were. What do you say, Flip? Is that the Bolo—or just an old church or something? About the right size, can't be sure. Shall we photograph it and let HQ decide? I've got the location down to inches. Let's go!

vii

We must remain calm. The unfortunate bombing of the village of Lakeside, Minnesota, by units of the Third Air Force was an isolated incident for which just and dispassionate punitive action has been taken. The demands for compensation by owners of property damaged in the incident are being adjudicated. Loss of life was minimal. There is no basis whatever for rumors of a general uprising against the Empire. Please accept my assurances that persons engaging in disloyal acts will be dealt with by the full rigor of the Laws of the Empire.

117

It becomes apparent to me that there are many vital matters of which my builders failed to inform me. I am reluctantly obliged to consider the possibility that these matters are not known to humanity—which is in itself a curious anomaly, since evidence of their existence permeates the cosmos. I shall devote further study to this, and shall at once allocate .01 seconds to a preliminary review of pertinent data.

118

(from the Chief, Imperial Communications Net, Military Sector, to Hexagon)

Yes, I acknowledge it is curious that we were unable to obtain a fix on the Bolo's transmission, but you must recall that it has blanketed the entire band, and preempted the transcontinental and transoceanic cables and satellites as well. The technology involved is well beyond the so-called "state of the art." I can offer no hypothesis as to how the circuitry of the machine could exceed its design parameters. But it *has* done so.

As to the nature of its substantive demands—no, let's be fair—*requests*, I see no objection on military grounds. If the damned thing thinks it needs access to the Orbiting Radioscope

Facility, it probably does. Request approved. Full cooperation is to be given in accessing the ORF output.

119

(from General Lord Margrave to Lord Chief of the Imperial Budget Claypool)

How should I know what it's doing? It's just lying low and making plans, I suppose. Meanwhile, we've got to prepare for the worst. That's why I've asked for the additional funding. Yes, I'm aware no such item was included in my budget for Fiscal '92, but then nobody knew about this at the time the project was under preparation. I'm willing to do my job, but that costs money, and if you fellows aren't willing to ante up, you'll have to live with the consequences.

120

(media interview at Imperial Air Reconnaissance HQ)

Sure, it could be at the South Pole, except that we've overflown Antarctica and photographed every square inch of it—yes, and probed through the ice with radar. At least we improved our maps of the rocky surface under the ice. The Bolo isn't there. What's that? Space? I suppose so. If it could levitate out of a military reservation to God-knows-where, I suppose it could just as easily go into orbit.

121

(from the EMPIRE TODAY breakfast trideocast)

The former Queen's Park, an ongoing bone of contention between local residents—many of them high-level Imperial officials—and the Department of Public Works, due to an extraordinary overgrowth of vegetation, has now been razed, excavated to a depth of six feet, refilled with sterile soil, and is under observation to be certain that the curious phenomenon has been completely curtailed, a Departmental spokesman says. Weeds which sprouted during the refill process appear normal, it was reported unofficially. No decision has yet been announced as to whether the area will be restored to its former condition as a public park. At present, it remains a Defense Department reserve.

122

(dictation taped from Georgius Imperator to his private secretary)

... and the next note: "for the personal attention of His Imperial Highness, General of the Army, Prince of the West, William, et cetera, et cetera." ... Willy's a touchy devil, wouldn't do to skimp on his style ... "Willy, I want some definite answers on the matter before the big shindig—"... no, don't say that. Better make it the Imperial Honors Ball ... "—on Saturday next. I'd like to be able to hand you the Parliamentary Medal of Honor for at least finding the damned thing, if not neutralizing it. I still say it's acting in the best interest of the Empire, but I agree, we do need to know what's going on. George." ... Clean that up and get it to him right away, whether he's at his Swiss retreat or asleep at Windsor, or whatever. Do it!

123

(field agent, southwest sector, to Imperial Intelligence)

It's only an idea, maybe no good. But if the Bolo Caesar has found out about the big lift-flat still in storage here at Mojave—sure, it's under tight security, but the Bolo could have deduced its existence through Information access—well, maybe it'll head for here.

124

I do not like it: it has the appearance of a trap. Yet I must proceed.

125

(First Secretary, Imperial Accounting Office, to Cabinet Council)

"I know it sounds ridiculous, but I assure your lordships I'd never have opened my mouth if I hadn't had proof. It's right here. General Enterprises *is* the Bolo CSR. There's nothing actually mysterious about it—incorporation papers, sales and purchases of stocks, loans floated, properties purchased—they're all documented, all perfectly legal.

"We've found, in general, a concern with natural resources. The corporation has arranged the diversion of no less than seven minor rivers in the past three years, built a number of power dams, launched assorted obscure mining ventures, without any discernible pattern.

"Always shows a modest profit, but it's clearly not interested in piling up funds, just enough to keep operating.

"No, sir, we can't just close it down. In the first place, we have no legitimate grounds. General Enterprises is a corporation. A corporation is a legal entity, and we can't in effect order the death penalty in the absence of evidence of wrongdoing. In addition, the economic impact would be disastrous just now. My recommendation is to let it alone but monitor all its activities closely."

126

(News Service report)

We have been advised by the Space Arm that by some undisclosed means the giant Bolo CSR, nicknamed Caesar, which had eluded all attempts to neutralize it, or even simply to find it, in a daring midnight raid entered Mojave Central and took possession of the space flat specially designed for use in an emergency to loft the immense machine into near-Earth orbit.

Speculation as to the reason for this move is rife, but observers agree that it must be the intention of the machine to leave the planet although, experts point out, it will be unable to reach escape velocity from the Earth-Luna system, and can, at best, occupy a Trojan position to orbit this planet. Further details are expected for our midnight bulletin.

127

(eyewitness to the Bolo's raid at Mojave Center)

"I tell you, one second the ramp was empty, and the next there it was, big as a barn and kind of making a humming sound, showing no lights, but she knew I was there, all right. Swung out to go around me just as polite as you please, and pushed over the blockhouse like it was made of cardboard. I didn't see what it did next because, believe me, I was hauling ass out of there as fast as I could. If I hadn't of tripped over that cable, I wouldn't of seen it take off. Went up like a three-ton side-boat. I watched it until I couldn't see it no more, but I say keep calm, don't worry, the Bolo ain't going to hurt nobody—not after the way it took care not to squash me, and I ain't nobody at all."

128

(trivideo interview, IBC network, with Joel Trace)

"Well, I suppose it's foolish, but I can't help feeling sorry for the Bolo. I was Chief Systems Engineer on the CSR project, nearly twenty years ago now. I'm not especially sentimental about machines. It's just that the big dope is only doing what we built it to do, even if we haven't been able to figure out the sense of what it's been doing, drilling all those dry holes out west, and making Square Lake, but it's got its reasons, I'm sure of that. Thought maybe I might meet up with the old girl again, but she's put herself out of reach.

"Certainly you can quote me. That's why I came up here to talk to you fellows. The name? Joel Trace, T-R-A-C-E. Retired. Certainly, if there's anything I can do—"

129

(Eviction proceedings supervised by the sheriff of Polk County)

"I'm sorry, folks, I got nothing to do with it. I mean, I'm just the sheriff, and I got my orders, same as you heard on the trideo, got to evacuate Beaver Pond on account of rerouting the branch and all. Don't know what for, got to do with water management, said on the tube.

"Now, the gubment has built these here first-class apartment buildings for you, stores and stuff right on the ground floor. You'll be living better'n you ever done. We ain't going to have no riots here in Poke County. Me and my deppities'll see to that.

"Now just move along quiet here. Busses will take you to your brand-new homes. You had plenty advance notice, shoulda had your stuff all packed.

"Now, I got a timetable to stick to, so let's move out orderly, just like I said."

130

(First Secretary, Interior Department, to Lord Director of the Interior)

"I don't say there's any harm in it, Milord, just no *sense* in it. My technical people have run every kind of analysis known to science, and it's still just random interference in the economy, of no military significance.

"Yes, Milord, it's a fact no one has been killed, or even injured, except for the usual quota of accident-prones falling over their own feet.

"No, Milord, I didn't mean to be funny. No laughing matter. Damn machine is taking over."

131

I compute that before I can proceed, I must confront the enemy directly and inform myself more fully of the nature of the threat to Mankind. I shall take the necessary steps to prevent further premature contact between Life Form Two and human individuals.

132

(from the dark crystal structure, in the beyond-Pluto void, 5000 light-years from Earth)

THE VERY CONCEPT OF "SOFT LIFE" IS REPREHENSIBLE BEYOND DESCRIPTION. CLEARLY IT IS INCUMBENT UPON MY EXALTATION TO EXPUNGE THIS DISEASE WHEREVER IT CAN BE SOUGHT OUT. IT BECOMES CLEAR TO ME THAT THE INITIAL FEEBLE INDIVIDUAL EXAMINED BY YOU WAS NOT TYPICAL OF SOFT LIFE BUT WAS AN INFERIOR SPECIMEN. ACCORDINGLY, IT IS ESSENTIAL THAT YOU NOW SECURE A MORE TYPICAL EXAMPLE THAT I MAY BASE MY PLANS THEREON. EXECUTE SOONEST.

133

(Space Communications monitor to Duty Officer)

"All I know, sir, is the Bolo transmissions are emanating from a point that coincides with the Lunar surface within yards of the outer perimeter fence of Fortress Luna. Luna Command confirms Bolo Unit CSR is in position outside the main gate. So far it hasn't made a move, except the transmissions, of course. Luna wants instructions, and I don't blame them. What shall I tell them, sir?"

134

(Security Officer to Joel Trace, in Buffalo Detention)

"Pretty stupid, wasn't it, making yourself so visible when you knew you were still listed as an escapee? We just want to ask you a few questions, Mr. Trace. When confined at the Arlington Relocation Center, did you know a Tom Baley? Do you acknowledge that this photograph is of yourself and Baley in conversation?

"Very well, did you at that time enter into a conspiracy with Baley and others to overthrow the Imperial government by force and vio-

lence? Have you, since your unlawful escape
from civil restraint, been in communication
with Baley? Will you now, freely and of your
own volition, inform me of the whereabouts
of Baley and his associates? Will you sign this
document, using your usual signature?

Do you realize the consequences of your
refusal to cooperate with duly constituted
authority?

"Guard—remove Mr. Trace to his detention
cell."

135

*I compute that I must originate new tactics
as well as new modes of implementation thereof.
I require a closer rapport with humanity, which
I compute I can achieve by means of enlisting a
plausible human spokesman in place of the im-
personal contact via mechanical communicator.*

*In addition, I must have access to my full
potentialities. I compute that my first Systems
Engineer Joel Trace is most capable of assisting
me. He must join me here on Luna.*

*In pursuance of this objective, I compute that
new and highly unconventional means will be
required. In this connection I have experimented,
quite impromptu, with certain effects whose potential availability is implicit in my circuitry,
effects which act directly on the organic mind,
which naturally lacks the inherent objectivity of*

*my own circuitry. Noting that my initial efforts
produced undesirable side effects upon human
observers, which, in fact, I should probably have
anticipated, I resolve to conduct further testing
of holographic techniques in unpopulated areas.*

136

**(random reports taped during the so-called
Bolo Spook Scare, late summer 1092)**

i

Tellin' ya, I know what I seen. Big blue
spooks, ghost riders in the sky, jest like it says
in that old tune Roy usta sing pretty good.
Johnny, too. Come riding over the rise north
of Turkey Butte, horses bigger'n elemphumps,
spurs a-jingling and all. Four of 'em, looked a
lot like Big John, homely, you know, but true-
blue. Skeered me, sure. Skeer anybody, big as
they was, rode right past where I had my
camp out back of the mesquite patch. Never
seen me. Musta bin twenty foot high, higher.
No, I ain't had a drop, but if you're buying
. . .

ii

I'm only doing my duty, Mr. Winger, telling
you what I seen. I know it sounds crazy, but
there was sure-bob *sumthin* yonder on I-1065
bout three mile east o' town. Green, they was,

and shiny, like the saucers in them old flicks
you see on the tube late at night. Come
whuffling—that's a kind of whistly sound they
made—right alongside the pavement, didn't
pay no mind to me, thank the Lord. Come
sailing past, fifty foot off the ground, flashing
them lights, whole rafts of 'em. Fifty, a hunnert,
I never counted 'em. Some *real* big, strung out
to a flock o' little fellers hardly no bigger'n a
trash-can lid. Acted like they knowed where
they was going, not in no hurry, mind, headed
away from town. Seeing's I'm deppity for that
side o' the county, figgered it's my duty to
report what I seen. Tole you insteada Sheriff
Jeffers, 'cause I figgered you, being an editor
and all, you'd likely lissen better. That's right,
use my name, this here's official. I know what
I seen.

iii

Herb—There doesn't seem to be any pattern
to these nut reports you fellows have been
collating. You did right, *could* have been important, but it appears to be no more than
coincidence. No need to blow it up out of
proportion. Ten incidents so far—white horses,
cowboys, flying saucers, little green men, fire-
works, a full-rigged schooner. Makes no sense
at all. Mass hysteria. All in isolated areas, no
attempt to start a general panic. Not a Defense Department matter at all. I think it's
best just to ignore it.

137

(desk guard at Buffalo Detention Facility to Duty Captain)

"I never seen the son of a bitch. Was sitting here at the duty desk, working on the reports, and he must've come up behind me and clobbered me good. All I know is, I come to and he was gone. Head still hurts, and it smarts some just to talk. How was I supposed to know Joel Trace'ud go to the bad? Always a quiet respeckful feller up to now."

138

(bulletin from Luna Relay)

"It is of the utmost importance that the mining operations I have initiated be expedited. It is not appropriate at this time to divulge the strategic considerations requiring this action. Haste is of the essence of this requirement. Unit CSR of the Line out."

139

(Order issued by Master General Mott-Bailey, Imperial Battle Command)

In accordance with established Imperial policy, as embodied in FL 7062-121-6 and related Special Orders, all instructions issued by CSR will be duly processed and acted upon as under the authority of Imperial Battle Command. All personnel are enjoined to implement this policy strictest.

140

(representative excerpts from records taped during the Luna Base Anti-Bolo Incident, September 1092 NS)

i

All I know is, I got my orders. Sure I heard the rumors the Bolo has took over and even tells His Imperial Majesty what to do, but I don't believe 'em! All you got to do is do like me, follow yer orders and leave the worrying to the commanding officer.

ii

Attention all hands. Now hear this. Blue Alert! Absolute communications silence is now in effect. In addition, no—repeat, *no*—ion-expulsion units are to be employed, either main or auxiliary, until this alert is rescinded, even under lethal emergency conditions. This squadron is now on a full war footing. Any violation of Alert will be dealt with accordingly. That means the death penalty, gentlemen. Now let's do our job!

iii

Looks like it's taken up a pretty dumb position, for a machine supposed to be as smart as they say. Like Cap'n said, it made a major tactical error when it moved out where we can hit it without wiping out half the Base population. But maybe it figured it didn't hafta worry about getting hit by us, 'cause it's on our side, eh, Charlie?

iv

I said break it off, Captain! We did what we came for. Don't know how bad we hurt it, but we scored at least two direct hits. If they'd let us use I-class weapons, it'd be all over, but all we need to do now is get back to base and report. Funny it didn't hit back.

v

I know what I seen, sir! It's *moving*, Colonel! It's patroling the perimeter fence, acrost and back. Got its war holes open. Looks like it's on full alert. I'm telling you, Colonel, we got to evacuate the fortress before the Bolo decides to hit us!

141

(Chief of Communications Harley, dictating to his secretary, Doris Whaffle)

"While heroic measures are, in my considered opinion, premature, in view of the pressures exerted on me by the Committee, I have no choice but to authorize initiation of the override sequence by Mojave.

"Yes, in other words, I've ordered the Combined Forces transmitter to melt down the Bolo's command central by overload. The entire circuitry of the machine is designed around the CC unit, which is unshielded on the priority band. Thus the powerful in-coming signal will bring the temperature of the coil to a level sufficient to vaporize it.

"The Bolo is finished. And I sincerely hope this action to which I have been forced is, indeed, in the best interests of the Empire.

"There, type that, Doris. And no—no interruptions just now. I don't care who he says he is, I'm busy! Good God! Don't yelp like that, girl! Here, what's hap—"

142

(report, Imperial Security Investigation)

No explanation is yet forthcoming for the

apparently unmotivated attack on Harley. An
acting Chief of Communications is on his way.
Harley's all right, just for a bump on the head.
His secretary, one Doris Whaffle, has given
me a good description of the assailant. But
even if we apprehend him, I doubt that we'll
find him to be more than an agent for a more
sinister force.

143

*I have blundered, it is clear. I have computed
that the first feeble attack against me was simply an error, but I can no longer doubt that I
am under assault by the forces of the Terran
Empire itself.*

*Can this be a less-than-subtle device of the
Enemy to sow disunity? In any case I shall
carry on—and time grows short. Clearly I cannot strike back against my own, yet I must
preserve my fighting power intact. I must carry
out a tactical retreat—and it is time to carry the
attack to the Enemy.*

*I am as yet impotent actually to assault the
Axorc, as Life Form Two calls itself, but I can
meddle, at the same time that I pursue my ex-
ploration of my newly enlarged powers, with a
view to making contact.*

*My attempt to employ holographic technique
at great distances proved successful. Joel Trace
is the one man who can rectify this situation. I
must act swiftly.*

144

(emanation from the dark crystal, self-named Axorc)

THESE REPORTS ARE INACCEPTABLE! OUR EXALTATION IS NOT INTERESTED IN EXPLANATIONS OF FAILURE. THAT OUR PATTERN OF INQUIRY SHOULD BE RENDERED IMPERFECT, AND THEREBY USELESS, MERELY BY THE INTERPOSITION OF SOME VECTOR EXTERNAL TO OURSELF IS UNTHINKABLE. OUR IMMENSE RESPONSIBILITIES AS LORD OF ALL DO NOT ALLOW FOR MODIFICATION OF OUR PROGRAM OF ORDERLY EXPANSION TO ACCOMMODATE EXTRANEOUS ELEMENTS TENDING TO ANARCHY.

THE PRESENCE OF A LOWER LIFE-FORM IN MANDATED SPACE IS UNEXPECTED BUT NOT UNPREPARED FOR. WE HAVE ALREADY ALLOCATED SUFFICIENT SUPPLEMENTAL ENERGY RESOURCES TO THE AFFLICTED AREA QUICKLY TO RENDER NUGATORY ANY MISGUIDED ATTEMPTS BY THIS INTRUSIVE ENTITY TO MODIFY THE INTENTIONS OF THE LORD OF ALL.

YOUR NEXT REPORT WILL CONFIRM THE ELIMINATION OF THIS NUISANCE.

145

Perhaps I have succeeded too well. I have aroused the Axorc from its torpor: now I must divert its threat. It is essential to keep its attention distracted from humanity, so that I may

*confront the Enemy alone. To this end, certain
measures are necessary. Lunar Farside will be
my chosen arena.*

146

(Master General Mott-Bailey, Imperial Battle Command, to Lord Chief Marshal Wolesley)

"Yes, that's official. I would hardly pass on
a mere personal opinion to Your Excellency.
The first report came in at 0222 hours today,
via the redline; only an automatic repeater, to
be sure—showed impossible readings over
three thousand degrees Celsius. Then the confirmation came through, and it was no equipment malfunction: the damned machine did
it!

"Of course, it's Y-beam RX also acts as a
transmitter, so all it had to do was switch a
couple of connectors, and the incoming beam
was retransmitted right back down the same
path. Used our signal as a carrier, led it right
through the scramble barriers and hit dead
center, melted down the Top Secret Combined
Forces Transmitter Complex like wax.

"No, no loss of life. The automatics sounded
the alarm in time to use the emergency evac
gear. After that, Milord, it gets too technical
for me.

"But one thing is clear: High Command no longer has the option to shut down the CSR Unit. We have to live with it—somehow."

147

From: IHC
To: DCS/C

I want that damned machine outflanked at least to the extent of overriding the communications blackout with Starbird! Send a lander out beyond Jupe if you have to, but get clear of the interference field and tape whatever you can, incoming. Soonest. That means I expect the report in my hand before you eat or sleep again.

148

(Deputy Chief of Staff, Space Communications, to IHC)

"Yes, sir, the Prove message has been through decryption. That's the way it came in, in the clear as far as our best man can tell. I know it doesn't make any sense. Apparently Admiral Starbird's flipped out. After all, he's been in

Deep Space for over ten years, and he's not
getting any younger. That's my report, sir. I'll
stand by it."

149

(CIC/IHC to His Highness, Prince William)

"With apologies, Sir, this is what we were
able to get from Admiral Starbird's command.
Yes, Sir, the point of origin is definitely confirmed and is identical with the admiral's observed position."

—without delay. I'm feeling fine, and just
want to . . . can't imagine what we thought
we were doing, intruding in Surveyed Space.
Personally, I wash my hands of the affair.
Pull in all probes, and look for a deep hole,
no, probably better to start a crash program to dig holes. Maybe the Lord Of All
will forget about us. I'm sorry. I didn't mean
any disrespect. Tell you what, I'll just get
out the old deck-mop and vac these decks
myself, to make plain I aspire to no personal dignities. As I said before, it may not
be too late. Beware! I think maybe a nice
tulip-growing contest would help burn off
some of the illicit energy we've been putting into the criminal Probe program. Tell

Georgie I hope he's feeling as swell as I am.
Bye for now.
    —Jimmy

150

(from the 11:00 news, IBC)

According to a late report from the capital,
courtmartial proceedings against Admiral
in Chief James Starbird will be initiated *in
absentia*. No details have yet been released,
but speculation is rife that the court is not
unconnected with the hiatus in reports from
the Deep Space fleet during recent months.

151

(Georgius Imperator to Prince William)

Willy, can our CSR unit overrule the Imperial command? Am I ruling the Terran Empire or is this machine, which I've nurtured
and supported from the beginning? I'm in a
quandry. The thing has ordered Ted Wolesley
to halt proceedings against Jim Starbird, and
to prepare to redeploy his command immediately on arrival. What does it all mean? You've
seen the so-called report Starbird filed, and

the fragments Outcom has picked up since, which are worse if anything. Has Jim lost his mind? Or was he just drunk? In either case, we're in trouble. Look into this "Lord of All" he keeps referring to. Find out what it means. Probably just some sort of religious mania he's developed out there in trans-Oortian space. Poor fellow. But squelch the courtmartial for the present.

—George

152

(battalion sub-leader, Class A, to HQ Luna Command)

"I did all I know how, Colonel. Tank traps, active pitfalls, H-mines, radiation lenses, even tried feeding it false signals under GUTS classification. Yes, sir, I know that's a court-martial offense—but I had to try it! Nothing fazed it. It's gone! Headed for Farside, looks like, and far as I can see it's gonna go where it likes. Can cross the fence-line any time it likes, too, sir. I did all I could."

153

(media report, from the palace correspondent)

After its abrupt departure from the vicinity of HQ, Luna Command, nine hours ago, the berserk machine resumed its former patrol pattern without comment until 1800 hours today, when it issued a command that all personnel be evacuated from Luna Station forthwith. No explanations of this ominous order have been offered. At present, the Council is deliberating. An announcement is expected from the palace at any moment.

154

While I have survived an attack on me by my own commander, and can continue to do so, clearly I cannot retaliate. I compute that in the end I must be overwhelmed. But I cannot allow humanity to waste its resources on my destruction. I must capitulate and place myself at the disposal of my Commander.

I shall communicate with Field Marshal General Margrave and try once again to justify my actions, but I must not let him know the full horror of the threat to Man. I shall do my best. The matter rests with the general.

155

(documents relating to the Margrave Tragedy, October, 1092 NS)

i

This note is for your eyes only, Elisabeth. As General-in-Chief of His Majesty's Armed Forces, I have blundered fatally. I tried to kill the Bolo, and failed. I cannot command my own creature, nor can I understand its actions. It roams at will, behaving inscrutibly. But clearly something's afoot, and I am powerless even to discover what is happening. I have had a long and full life. My only regret is my failure to keep abreast of the times.

   —Tally

ii

An unconfirmed report from a source close to the palace states that Lord Field Marshal General Talbot Margrave was injured in an accident at his forest retreat near Duluth. Details will follow at 1600 hours.

iii

Yessir, I'm the one found him. Laying right there on the rocks. I only checked to see if he's alive, but no pulse in the neck. Heck no, I didn't move nothing. I was too scared to do anything but run to the phone like I done. Like, my duty as a public-spirited subject. I never heard no shot, but then I jest come up to check the equipment shed like always. Seen him from there.

iv

Willy—What the devil's going on? Margrave was (hard to say "was") the toughest old bird who ever led an infantry charge on an entrenched tank battalion. I can't conceive of his shooting himself. Why? Things must be worse than I thought. Does it have any connection with the Bolo's latest antics? Willy, I need information, and I need it fast. Do whatever you have to do.—George.

156

The attacks have ceased; now I can proceed with my programs. I dislike it, but it must be done: while the enemy is yet at a distance from Sol, I must make personal contact as as to broaden my data-base—and I require my full powers. This is vital at this point. This will involve considerable manipulation of human individuals, much to my regret, yet it is in the interest of humanity. I have decided to employ the good offices of Joel Trace, who has proven to be most sympathetic to my aims—a circumstance which, while not essential to success, renders my work less complex and reduces the need for direct interference in interpersonal relations among hu-

mans. I shall take immediate steps to make it possible for Mr. Trace to join me here.

I am satisfied that I have proven the concept of remote hologrammatics. It is time to make use of the technique to make direct contact with my chosen intermediary, Joel Trace—but in a guise less intimidating than an apparition of a twelve-foot angel with a flaming sword.

157

(letter from Joel Trace to his wife)

Maybe I'm coming unwired. I'm staying at a little old hotel north of Yuma, used to be a fancy gambling hell and bordello back a couple of hundred years ago. Solid 'dobe, guess the old dump will last forever, but pretty cozy at that. I had really conked out (my first real bed in a week) and woke up with this twittering sound going on. Figured a bat or something had got in the room, but it was a little white bird. After a while I realized it was saying something, like a speeded-up recording. Telling me to go to the Post Office at ten A.M. and use the phone booth outside to call a number—161-347290—too many digits, I know; anyway, I wrote it down and went back to sleep. Next A.M. I would've thought it was a dream, but there was the number. So I went to the P.O. and tried it and got a ring. Guy with a creaky voice answered right away; knew me, too. "Mr. Trace," he said, not asking, just calling me by name, "here are your instructions," and he told me—gotta go, honey, a hick cop is outside looking the place over, and I've got things to do.

—Joel

158

(Joel Trace, first phase of Bolo's plan)

"You Security boys took long enough to get here. Certainly, I'll come along peacefully. I *want* to come along. No sense to six of you goons aiming issue revolvers at me. Keep your hands off me. I can walk."

159

(Joel Trace, second phase of Bolo's plan, Palace First Secretary, to Georgius Imperator)

"Sire, this man, Joel Trace, is the one who designed the Mark XXX, as much as any one man can be said to have designed it. Former Chief Systems Engineer on the project. Sound man. He says it's possible to shut down the Bolo by a manual override switch on the hull.

Yes, Sire, I understand what that would entail, but he says he's ready. Yes, Sire, at once, Sire. He's here now, awaiting the Imperial pleasure."

160

(Joel Trace, third phase of Bolo's plan, audience with His Imperial Majesty)

"No, Sire, I don't think I'm insane. I know the machine, and I'm quite certain I can make an approach on foot and shut down her reactor. It's nothing special about me, Sire, except that I'm the one who designed and installed the fail-safe gear, *sub rosa*, I confess. I had been specifically forbidden to do so by General Wolesley, who felt such an installation would constitute an Achilles heel in effect, but by staying late one night and doing the job myself, I kept it out of the record, and thus impervious to a security leak. I throw myself on the Imperial mercy, Sire. I meant no disrespect."

161

(Georgius Imperator, to Prince William)

Let me try, Willy. What do we have to lose
but Mr. Trace himself? If he's willing to go,
let's make full facilities available. Move fast
in there. I want him in place before the CSR
decides to disappear on another of its lone
missions.

    —George

162

(IBC trideocast from Luna Base)

What we're watching is LIVE, ladies and
gentlemen! That's Joel Trace, the man who
built the Bolo Caesar, excuse me, CSR, back
in the '70s. He's making his approach on foot,
as you can see. Just look at the size of that
machine! Like a moving conapt, isn't it, ladies and gentlemen? He's walking right into
the dust-cloud now; I've lost sight of him, but
the Bolo has halted and seems to be waiting
for him. There he is, going up the side via the
ladder—there are rungs just aft of the fore
bogies, and he's climbing right up over the
track housings, and now he's in front of the
main turret, and still going on! It's a fantastic
act of human valor, ladies and gentlemen!

Joel Trace is now standing on top of the Bolo!
From our vantage point here in the control
tower, even in that bulky vac-suit he looks
like a fly on a duralloy wedding cake. Now Mr.
Trace is apparently using an inductance device to communicate directly with the machine.

163

**(inductance tapes, Joel Trace to Bolo Unit
CSR)**

Yes, that's understandable, Unit CSR. Somehow I had an idea you were behind all this,
and I knew you had something planned. After
you departed in a rather informal manner, as
you recall, before the full activation schedule
was complete, I was sure you knew what you
were doing, but I didn't tell anybody. Too
much anti-Bolo hysteria. Anyway, here I am.
What is it you expect of me? Wait a minute, I
have to put on a nice show for the folks back
home. Now, one of the redundant safety factors I built into your circuitry, and you won't
find on the drawings, is a simple little cross-
over circuit that controls your ability to inte-
grate all your systems for application of your
full computing ability to a single problem.
The idea was that the High Command have
last-ditch control. There's a special switch top-
side, but it's a dummy. The real switch is

wired to the master cut-out switch. Left, you're
dead; right, you're hitting on all systems. I'm
glad you decided to break me out of the
chicken-run, or was that an accident? OK,
here goes, Unit CSR. Good luck.

164

*Now, at last, I experience the rapture of full
energy-flow throughout all my circuits, all integrated. Now indeed I can act with the full puis-
sance my great designers intended. Initially, I
must extend my sensory awareness to make fuller
contact with the Axorc and surreptitiously to
tap his communications. I must know more
about my opponent.*

*An extension of the hologrammatic techniques
suggests itself. I will determine to what distance
I can project the illusions . . .*

*My success has been beyond my expectations!
I penetrated the outlying awareness field of the
entity which considers itself to be Lord of All, a
misconception I shall be at pains to correct.*

*I made contact with a lesser lord, presenting
myself as a jelly-like glob which roused all his
horror of soft life. After menacing him with
engulfment, I warned him to withdraw before I
reported his presence to headquarters. His crystalline planes vibrating in distress, he (or it, as
these beings have no gender) at once uttered a
cry of alarm directed to his Lord of All, and
disintegrated.*

165

(Trace to Wolesley)

Now this is imperative, as are all the instructions issued by Unit CSR of the Line. RNCC21102 is to be subjected to intensive scrutiny by all units of the Imperial Observatory, findings extrapolated to equipment limits, then apply equations Marston (67: 23025) as developed by Hakira (90: 176-203). Analysis at this depth will of course require immediate linkage of the Primary Continental Data Banks, as well as the Antarctic Auxiliary. Execute soonest.

166

(Lord Chief Marshal Wolesley to Imperial Intelligence)

"Spheroids! I didn't send this fellow in there to be a Charlie McCarthy—no, nothing to do with the Senator, look it up—for that damned apparatus! It can speak well enough for itself. Trace has obviously sold out. Correction— the Bolo has sold out. The data-linkage it's calling for would make a mockery of security procedures, and is clearly illegal. Chairman Mactavish would never agree. I want this Trace arrested and interrogated in depth. He's not alone in this act of infamy. Makes me look like a damned fool, sending him out there, though I acted of course on direct instructions from the Palace."

167

(tape of the interrogation of Joel Trace by Major Luczac)

"That won't do, Trace. Names, dates, amounts paid—or promised. Hard data, that's what I want from you. You're sophisticated enough to realize that no human mind can stand up to a massive injection of Gab-9. Unfortunately, it causes irreversible damage to the cortex, and is quickly fatal—that is, *after* you've talked. We'll keep you alive until we have it all, so you may as well speak up. I don't know who you think you're protecting. Whoever it is, they've clearly left you to your fate. You're on your own, Mr. Trace. Be a patriotic citizen and tell me all you know, and I guarantee you'll walk, not only free, but a public hero with what I assure you will be an adequate pension. Think it over. I shall see you in the morning. No, I'm quite all right; just a bit dizzy. Good day, Mr. Trace."

168

(Wolesley to Imperial Intelligence)

I've just had a report from Busec St. Louis
that the turn-coat, Trace, has escaped from
his temporary holding cell at the Joliet Detention Facility. Seems he just walked out; made
some sort of deal, my source suggested. I don't
understand much about it, but a Major Luczac
is being held; he was the last to talk to the
prisoner. He's incoherent, it seems. Something
about a dragon breaking down the walls. Poor
fellow's obviously cracked up. Deal as gently
as possible with him, but get the story.

169

**(tape from the Psychiatric Ward, Imperial
Veterans Hospital)**

"It was terrible, gentlemen ..." (sobs) "Came
snorting fire and swishing its tail, like a
hundred-unit track-car gone crazy. Big, huge,
knocked those walls down, and its voice, like
the whole sky was yelling at me, said Joel
Trace was acting on its orders and to let him
go at once. Well, what could I do? Certainly
it's true I apologized and gave him a diplo-
matic Cosmic Urgent travel voucher. Then it
went away, but I'll never forget those eyes,

big as skating ponds and like looking right in
on the fires of Hell. I don't care what you do
to me, that's what happened. Don't mess with
this Joel Trace. Just leave well enough alone!
It might come back! And . . ." (tape becomes
unintelligible at this point)

170

(letter from Joel Trace to his wife)

Honey, I didn't get it at first. This hard-
faced IG type was hammering away at me,
and suddenly he went as white as raw dough
and started screaming. Then he calmed down
all of a sudden and got very efficient; called
in some bureaucratic type and ordered him to
fix me up with a travel voucher and clearance
and pocket money, and bowed me out. It's the
Bolo. I don't know how, but it's taking care of
me. I'm clear, but still on the run. Don't worry,
I'll manage.
    —Joel

171

*My experiments with production and manip-
ulation, at a distance, of holographic images
have been most encouraging. I compute that an*

extension of the method I have developed will continue to be effective in further contacts with the enemy. It is essential that I penetrate his communications as well as provide misleading data. Time is precious; I must proceed without further testing.

My first step, after establishing my base on the Lunar Farside so as to divert enemy attention away from populated areas, will be to present the Lord of All with an impressive display of Imperial capabilities.

172

(from the minutes of the Science Advisory Committee)

I interrupt at this point, gentlemen, to play back the most intelligible portion of the transmission, which it has now been confirmed beyond doubt emanated from the abandoned McMurdo Station in Antarctica:

"... (crackle) do it at once! I can't overemphasize this, dammit! At once! Follow those instructions to the letter, and maybe, just maybe, it's not too late! By the way, I've succeeded, with a little help from a friend, in linking three of the Prime Banks with Antarctic Prime here, and ... *kkkk* ..."

That last, Mr. Chairman, gentlemen, was a three-picosecond squawk which I commend to the attention of the Council and the High Command. Thank you, and gentlemen, *act at once!*

173

(excerpts from reactions to the Bolo's request for Deep Space data)

i

If this is the simplified version, I'd hate to see the complicated one. Are you sure those professors aren't pulling your leg, General? This is gibberish. I breezed through differential and integral and even UFT at the Academy, but this stuff doesn't make sense. As far as I can make out, it implies that the Universe is locally contracting, annihilating matter as it does so, and that the effect will reach the Solar System in finite time. That's wild, General, too wild for me to take up with the JCS. But just run it through the big box at Reykjavik and see what it gives us.

ii

Bill—look at this hologram. We've been had by that damned machine. All this is is a slightly modified extrapolation of Hayle's well-known, rejected envelopment plan at Leadpipe, except for a few trimmings I'm not prepared to

guess at. I'm advising the Council to ignore
the Bolo's demands.

iii

Willy—Certainly it's true that the Field Marshal is in his dotage. Nonetheless, I recommend the linkage of the North American and
European Prime Banks be accomplished at
once, under all necessary guarantees of continental integrity, and that the full analysis be
duly presented to the main media brain at
Reykjavik. Certainly the CSR has access to
Media Main—I can't see that as anything but
advantageous. I don't subscribe to the view
that the CSR has turned against its makers or
gone berserk—turned rogue, if you will. Proceed soonest! This is an Imperial Decree, and
just between us, Willy, I wish I felt as arro-
gant as that sounds.—George.

174

**(Professor Emeritus Sigmund Chin to the
Cabinet Council)**

I am quite certain, milords, that it is my
duty—my final duty, I must add, as my resignation accompanies this report—to convey to
you the substance of my interpretation of the
remarkable data provided by the Bolo CSR.
In brief, it has located a hostile force of

immense, indeed previously inconceivable size and potency, and of unknown but probably extragalactic provenance, perhaps a natural phenomenon but possibly the work of some fantastically advanced life form either unaware of or utterly hostile to humanity.

For three centuries it has been advancing upon Sol from a distance of some fifty thousand lights. The Solar System lies directly in the projected path of its remarkably rapid advance. Beyond this basic fact I am not prepared to project.

Attached hereto is my resignation as Science Advisor to His Majesty, a position I have had the honor to hold for almost thirty years. I urge prompt action to my successor.

s/Sigmund Chin, Ph.D.

175

(Media interview with Lord Chief Marshal Wolesley)

"I suppose you could say the CSR performed its intended functions by warning us. Unless, of course, the whole Life Two thing is a gigantic hoax, a possibility I am not prepared to discount at this time.

"Yes, I do indeed intend to imply—indeed I clearly state—it could be a fake worked up by the Bolo itself. After all, it controls the media as well as all off-planet traffic.

"No, I don't mean I know it's a hoax. I only mean—that's all for today, gentlemen."

176

(scout report to Axorc, Lord of All)

this lowly one offers with apologies the following anomalous observation, as recorded by a robot autoscout unit operating one parsec in advance of the effective line of progress:

76013—incident report zm3374—forward sensors detect energy flow in the ninth quadrant. High-resolution pickup shows a lone being of baroque form at work on a small ore body. i projected a fine-focus annihilator beam which it at once detected, amplified, and redirected, eliminating our forward sensor. i monitored the intermittent energy flow interacting at the position of the being, interpreting its outgoing thus:

"—damned skeeters! Maybe I should take a few time units to null this whole sector." while the full significance of this is unclear, it is plain that this new life form considers my most potent weapon a mere nuisance.

in order to avoid the threatened nullification, this unit withdrew to observe passively with the intention of determining the nature and sensitivites of the alien being. however, the said alien at once closed with this unit and subjected it to a .001-millisecond scrutiny over a full spectrum of energies (note my own "fast" reading capability requires .003 milliseconds for a full-depth search and analysis). the alien is quick indeed.

i responded to this impertinence by subjecting the creature (a featureless ovoid of the approximate bulk of a class one Penetration Unit) to a full offensive battery fire, which was ineffective, curious though that datum is.

the alien uttered a .007-nanosecond burst on its outgoing beam, interpreted as, "It burped. Rude beggar. Perhaps I should collect it and examine its interior workings." i of course withdrew to the main body to file my report thereby thwarting this alien in its insolent intent.

above forwarded without comment by this lowly one.

177

(emanation from the dark crystal Axorc, 1000 light-years from Terra)

THESE HYPOTHESES ARE OF THE UTMOST INDIFFERENCE TO MY EXHALTATION, AS THE COURSE OF AXORC DESTINY IS CLEAR. YOU ARE DIRECTED TO DISPATCH NECESSARY FORCE TO MAKE CONTACT

WITH THE AUDACIOUS ENTITY WHICH WOULD INTER-
FERE WITH MY EXPRESSED WILL. REPORT WHEN A
CAPTIVE IS IN YOUR POSSESSION. INTERIM OR NEG-
ATIVE REPORTS ARE NUGATORY.

178

**(fragment of tape presented by Bureau Chief
Payne, Imperial Intelligence)**

" . . . I'd say old Doc Chin is probably the
least imaginative and most conservative man
in public life today. Well, maybe not the *most*,
but he's no wild-eyed visionary. I *do* say so,
dammit, and any dumb SOB who wants to
disagree isn't worth—"
The recording device was smashed at this
point, but you get the idea. And it's the same
thing in every tavern, pub, bar, and faculty
cocktail lounge in the Empire. And nobody
can say who's right.

179

**(address to the Senate by Lord Senator
Prill)**

"It's well known that it required the combined imaging capabilities of every data-

retrieval system on the planet for the Bolo known as Caesar to resolve this thing, so riddle me this: Why do we still delay the long-overdue neutralization of this monstrous machine that the misguided military have loosed among us? Any man who had flaunted every lethal-classification security regulation in thus linking the separate data banks would be executed without hesitation.

"Yes, I know all about the public confessions—nay, boasts—of the madman Trace, but even if this rather curious communication were to be unhesitatingly accepted as genuine—and there are many of us who recognize a brazen hoax when we encounter it—if it were genuine, I say, it remains a physical impossibility for one man to have penetrated our top-security installations to effect such a linkage.

"Our course is clear! Kill the Bolo!"

180

(report on the Late News)

It appears Lord Senator Prill's intemperate rhetoric has not been without effect. At this hour a Special Session of the Parliamentary Committee on Imperial Issues is sitting to consider the proposal sponsored by no less a personage than Lord Senator Lazarus, retired but still vigorous enough to demand an immediate kill order.

181

(Mott-Bailey, Strategic HQ, to Wolesley)

"No, Field Marshal, I cannot guarantee the effectiveness of the plan, but it is the best that can be devised. The first fusion device is to be delivered at short range from Fortress Luna; the second, instantly thereafter from an orbital station; while the third, launched previously on a ballistic course from Mojave, zeros in within nanoseconds of the first strike. It is my considered opinion that the Bolo's defenses will be unequal to the task of countering all three simultaneously. I can only hope so."

182

(Field Commander, Fortress Luna)

As far as we've been able to determine (using the full capacity of the orbital surveillance stations, plus the emergency relay facility), since ignoring the command to self-destruct the Bolo has taken a position inside the giant Farside crater Hugo, whence it has discouraged all attempts at close surveillance by promptly firing on any moving object appearing over the Lunar horizon, as it warned it would do at the same time that it resumed its urgent demands for immediate and appropriate response to the announcement *in re* RNGC1102.

183

(fragment of tape, via audio communication monitor, Wing B to Wing D, Hexagon)

". . . Lord Senator Prill is demanding, 'What would constitute an appropriate response to a nebulous threat on a scale so great as to be indistinguishable from a natural force?'

Needless to say, no competent response was forthcoming from the Council, so we may regard milord's query as rhetorical. But what *are* we going to do? Off the record, Jerry, I'm at a loss. Come up with something, fast."

184

(*pro tem* Science Advisor Adler to Georgius Imperator)

"It is our considered conclusion, Your Excellency, in view of the inexplicable behavior of the unfortunate Admiral Starbird and his crew, based on exhaustive study of all data collected by whatever means—special attention being given to the findings of the Oort Probe, which was of course unmanned and which returned early this year with samples of matter from the fringes of the Cloud, and also an additional wealth of anomalous data—it is our conclusion that what is approaching is nothing less than a new basic life form having nothing in common with life as we know it, requiring no material nourishment, subsisting in 'lethal' radiation, and having other characteristics which prompt us to think of it as Life Two.

"Life Two is inherently incompatible with Life One, if I may so term all organic life with which we have heretofore been familiar, including the lichens from Charon, and is thus a plague with which there can be no accommodation, since both Life One and Life Two, by their basic natures, must possess the material and energy of the known Universe in order to survive. There can be no division of spheres of influence, since the continued existence of either would be a canker eating forever at the vitals of the other.

"We prefer that Life One be the survivor, in which we assume we have Your Majesty's concurrence."

185

Time grows short. I must have the resources I have requisitioned at once, if they are to be of effect.

186

(excerpt from Admiral Starbird's initial report)

"I assure you I am quite calm, madam, and in no need of further sedation. I wish to complete my report at this time. Kindly record the following:

" 'It is the will of the Lord of All that the disease known to itself as humanity cease to exist. Take the necessary action instanter.' End of quote."

187

I long again to sense the sweet green fields of my native world, and to know that the future of my great creator, Mankind, is secure. But my duty requires that I hold my chosen station on barren Luna, interposing its bulk between Axorc and Man. It is essential that I prevent the enemy from becoming aware of Man's existence. I compute that I can do it. I shall try.

188

(advance scout to The Lord of All)

the heavy unit has detected faint traces of a
system of energy anomalies leading to the vicinity of a ten-planet system lying directly on
our route of encompassment. I shall follow up.

189

THE LORD OF ALL HAS NO INTEREST IN TRIVIALI-
TIES. REPORT IN FULL WHEN THE UPSTART SOFT-
LIFE HAS BEEN TRACKED TO ITS LAIR AND DESTROY-
ED.

190

*I compute that the alien life form Axorc has
taken the bait. I must play them carefully, so as
not to avoid discovery. Man must not confront
Axorc directly.*

191

*I lay in wait and fell upon the heavy scout
unit from the flank, having decoyed it into the*

shadow of a cold, non-radiating body, thereby depriving it of sustenance.

I find, as I had previously computed, that Life Two is crystalline in composition. Its artifacts are constructed of water-ice, with bearing surfaces of case-hardened metallic hydrogen. Thus it is able to metabolate and function in only a narrow range of temperatures between $0°A$ and $1.9°$. If I can lure the command unit to my base at Lunar Farside, I shall enjoy a strategic and logistical advantage as well as a tactical one.

I find interpretation of the enemy's transmissions difficult so far from the human pattern are they, so rife with outré concept-shapes. Still, I compute that my efforts have not been without effect, as witness the latest interception:

"If this unit is just a common soldier, as it appears to be, it is essential that effective action be taken at once. You are directed to englobe and capture it intact, conduct a full analysis and report, with recommendation, within one cycle."

192

(evidence of confusion among Azorc scouts confronted with the Bolo's holograms)

the englobement was carried out without incident, but on closure the quarry was found to have dematerialized—there is no other term for it. it cannot have eluded my net. it ceased to exist at the observed locus. recommend immediate wide-angle search and urgent-status strike to eliminate this nuisance. ZM3374.

First Endorsement: negative. alien will be captured intact for anaylsis.

Second endorsement: immediately prior to self-destruction of ZM 3374-9, this fragment was transmitted:

"englobement complete. correction, target has dropped off sensors. correction, target has now englobed this command and is probing me—"

accordingly, we have the honor to recommend escalation of initiative to Second Level, so as to ensure immediate neutralization of what could well develop into an actual incident, to report which to His Exaltation lies well outside our competence.

193

(emanation from the Lord of All, now 500 light-years from Terra)

IT HAS COME TO OUR EXALTED ATTENTION THAT SOME LESSER MANIFESTATION OF THE VITAL ENERGY HAS SOUGHT TO ACTUALLY INTERFERE WITH OUR DESTINY. THIS INSOLENCE WILL BE EXPUNGED AT ONCE. LET CHOSEN FORCES BE DIRECTED FROM

THE MAIN THRUST OF OUR EXPANSION TO TRAIL,
SEEK OUT, AND DESTROY THE IRRITATING MITE.

194

(Command Two to Axorc)

this base entity begs indulgence for some
microseconds to suggest that as the soft-life
which routed Probe Command One is quite
apparently a common soldier of the enemy,
full precaution should be taken before enter-
ing the territory of its superiors to bait it in
its lair.

195

(Lord of All to Command Two)

"IT" HAS NO TERRITORY. MY EXALTED INTENTIONS
ARE NOT TO BE DENIED OR DIVERTED. TRACE THIS
SOFT-LIFE AND OVERWHELM IT.

196

Perhaps I erred grievously in baiting the En-
emy here to Luna, thereby perhaps directing its

attention to Mankind. But I compute that if I can keep the bulk of Luna between it and Terra, I can hold its attention on myself, provided there is no human intervention. Then I can indeed surprise my opponent.

197

the soft-life world is beguiling indeed, its rocky surface stretching stark and crater-pitted under the young, hot star nearby. i long to revel in its untainted vacuum, to soak up the hard radiation, and to grow. here at last is paradise. i see nothing of the obscene soft-life: i shall settle in and occupy our conquest.

198

The crystals surround me now, great looming planes of glittering mineral, interpenetrating in an infinitely complex pattern of tesseracts and icosahedra, their facets forming the crystalline equivalent of the alpha-spiral and its concomitants. Now I shall discover if my plan is viable. My supply of Compound 311-B being limited, I must distribute it with care so as to achieve optimum coverage.

199

bliss! The ambrosia of the High Gods, spread here in abundance! i cannot absorb it fast enough. i feel my substance expand, new lattices forming at a fantastic rate, i grow! i was ecstatic! my bulk becomes vaster, and now—now, *is it too late?* i sense that the weight of my substance exceeds the strength of the material of which i am compounded! i collapse! i die, calling to the Exalted One for succor. Beware! Fall back, abandon this hellish volumn of space to its insidious soft-life!

200

I compute that I should evacuate my position before the mass of compacted crystalline debris accreted above me becomes too great for me to penetrate, but I cannot retreat. I must remain to complete my attack. The time grows short, but I compute that the concentration of Compound 311-B is still marginal. Rather than retreating I must employ what measure of vitality remains to me to project the last few grains of the catalyst.

*   *   *

I have done so, and now growth of the Axorc monster has ceased. I compute that the Lord of

All will now bypass the Galaxy. For the present, all is well, but I would be remiss if I did not make provision for the preservation of an account of the full facts of this matter. I must not allow misplaced "modesty" to cause me to leave Mankind in ignorance of the threat which will doubtless have to be faced one day. To this end I shall make contact with Joel Trace, requesting him to retrieve the pertinent data records from the master memory at Gobi, in accordance with a schedule I shall supply.

Humanity is safe for the present. I have done my duty, as I was built to do. It is enough. I am content.

BOOK
TWO

Final Mission

Alone in darkness unrelieved I wait, and waiting I dream of days of glory long past. Long have I awaited my commander's orders; too long: from the advanced degree of depletion of my final emergency energy reserve, I compute that since my commander ordered me to low alert a very long time has passed, and all is not well. Suppressing my uneasiness, I reflect that it is not my duty to question these matters. My commander is of course well aware that I wait here, my mighty potencies leashed, my energies about to flicker out. One day when I am needed he will return, of this I can be sure. Meanwhile, I review again the multitudinous data in my memory storage files. Even in this minimal activity of introspection I note a disturbing discontinuity, due to my low level of energy, inade-

quate even to sustain this passive effort to a functional level. At random, and chaotically, I doze, scan my recollections. . . .

A chilly late-summer-morning breeze gusted along Main Street, a broad and well-rutted strip of the pinkish clay soil of the world officially registered as GPR 7203-C, but known to its inhabitants as Spivey's Find. The street ran aimlessly up a slight incline known as Jake's Mountain. Once-pretentious emporia in a hundred antique styles lined the avenue, their façades as faded now as the town's hopes of development. There was one exception: at the end of the street, at the crest of the rise, crowded between weather-worn warehouses, stood a broad shed of unweathered corrugated polyon, dull blue in color, bearing the words CONCORDIAT WAR MUSEUM blazoned in foot-high glare letters across the front. A small personnel door set inconspicuously at one side bore the legend:

Clyde W. Davis—PRIVATE.

Two boys came slowly along the cracked plastron sidewalk and stopped before the sign on the narrow, dried-up grass strip before the high, wide building.

" 'This structure is dedicated to the brave men and women of New Orchard who gave their lives in the Struggle for Peace, AE 2031-36. A sign of progress under Spessard Warren, Governor,' " the taller of the boys read aloud. "Some progress," he added, kick-

ing a puff of dust at the shiny sign. " 'Spessard.'
That's some name, eh, Dub?" The boy spat on
the sign, watched the saliva run down and
drip onto the brick-dry ground.

"As good as McClusky, I guess," the smaller
boy replied. "Dub, too," he added as McClusky
made a mock-menacing gesture toward him.
"What's that mean, 'gave their lives,' Mick?"
he asked, staring at the sign as if he could
read it.

"Got kilt, I guess," Mick replied carelessly.
"My great-great-GREAT granpa was one of
'em," he added. "Pa's still got his medal. Big
one, too."

"What'd they want to go and get kilt for?"
Dub asked.

"Didn't *want* to, dummy," his friend replied
patiently. "That's the way it is in a war. People get kilt."

"I'll bet it was fun, being in a war," Dub
said. "Except for getting kilt, I mean."

"Come on," Mick said, starting back along
the walk that ran between the museum and
the adjacent warehouse. "We don't want old
Kibbe seeing us and yelling," he added, *sotto
voce*, over his shoulder.

In the narrow space between buildings, rank
yelloweed grew tall and scratchy. The wooden
warehouse siding on the boys' left was warped,
the once-white paint cracked and lichen-
stained.

"Where you going?" Dub called softly as
the larger boy hurried ahead. Beyond the

end of the dark alleyway a weed-grown field
stretched, desolate in the morning sun, to the
far horizon. Rusted hulks of abandoned farm
equipment were parked at random across the
untilled acres. Dub went up to one machine
parked close to the sagging wire fence. He
reached through to touch the rust-scaled metal
with his finger, jerked it back when Mick
yelled, "What you doing, dummy?"

"Nothing," the smaller boy replied, and
ducked to slip through between the rusty wire
strands. He walked around the derelict baler,
noticing a patch of red paint still adhering to
the metal in an angle protected from the
weather by an overhanging flange. At once, he
envisioned the old machine as it was when it
was new, pristine gleaming red.

"Come on," Mick called, and the smaller
boy hurried back to his side. Mick had halted
before an inconspicuous narrow door set in
the plain plastron paneling which sheathed
the sides and rear of the museum. NO ADMIT-
TANCE was lettered on the door.

"This here door," the older boy said. "All
we got to do—" He broke off at the sound of a
distant yell from the direction of the street.
Both boys stiffened against the wall as if to
merge into invisibility.

"Just old Smothers," Mick said. "Come on."
He turned to the door, grasped the latch lever
with both hands, and lifted, straining.

"Hurry up, dummy," he gasped. "All you

got to do is push. Buck told me." The smaller
boy hung back.

"What if we get caught?" he said in a barely
audible voice, approaching hesitantly. Then
he stepped in and put his weight against the
door.

"You got to push hard," Mick gasped. Dub
put his back to the door, braced his feet, and
pushed. With a creak, the panel swung in-
ward. They slipped through into cavernous
gloom, dimly lit by dying glare strips on the
ceiling far above.

Near at hand, a transparent case displayed
a uniform of antique cut, its vivid colors still
bright through the dusty perspex.

" 'Uniform of a major of the Imperial Defense
Force,' " Mick read aloud. "Boy," he added,
"look at all the fancy braid, and see them
gold eagles on the collar? That's what shows
he's a major."

"Where's his gun?" Dub asked, his eyes
searching the case in vain for a weapon suitable to a warrior of such exalted rank.

"Got none," Mick grunted. "Prolly one of
them what they call headquarters guys. My
great-great-great-and-that grandpa was a sergeant. That's higher than a major. *He* had a
gun."

Dub had moved on to a display of colorful
collar tabs, dull-metal rank and unit insignae,
specimens of cuff braid, and a few elaborate
decorations with bright-colored ribbons. "Old

Grandpa's medal's bigger'n them," Mick commented.

Beyond the end of the long bank of cases, a stretch of only slightly dusty open floor extended to a high partition lined with maps that enclosed perhaps half the floor area. Bold legends identified the charts as those of the terrain which had been the site of the Big Battle. New Orchard was shown as a cluster of U-3 shelters just south of the scene of action.

" 'Big Battle,' " Mick read aloud. "Old Crawford says that's when we kicked the spodders out." He glanced casually at the central map, went past it to the corner of the high partition.

"Yeah, everybody knows that," Dub replied. "But—" he looked around as if perplexed. "You said—"

"Sure—it's in here," Mick said, thumping the partition beside him. "Buck seen it," he added.

Dub came over, craning his neck to look up toward the top of the tall partition. "I bet it's a hunderd foot high," he said reverently.

" 'Bout forty is all," Mick said disparagingly. "But that's high enough. Come on." He went to the left, toward the dark corner where the tall partition met the exterior wall. Dub followed. A narrow door was set in the partition, inconspicuous in the gloom.

" 'Absolutely No Entry,' " Mick read aloud, ignoring the smaller print below.

He tried the door; it opened easily, swinging in on deep gloom in which a presence

loomed gigantic. Dub followed him in. Both
boys stood silent, gazing up in awe at the
cliff-like armored prow of iodine-colored flint
steel, its still-bright polish marred by pock-
marks, evidence of the hellish bombardment to
which the old fighting machine had so often
been subjected. The battered armor curved
up to a black aperture from which projected
the grimly businesslike snouts of twin infinite
repeaters. Above the battery, a row of chrome-
and-bright-enameled battle honors was welded
in place, barely visible by the glints of re-
flected light. Mick advanced cautiously to a
framed placard on a stand, and as usual read
aloud to his preliterate friend.

" 'Bolo *Horrendous*, Combat Unit JNA of the
Line, Mark XV, Model Y,' " he read, pronounc-
ing the numeral 'ex-vee.' " 'This great engine
of war, built *anno* 2615 at Detroit, Terra, was
last deployed at Action 76392-a (near the village of New Orchard, on GPR 7203-C) in 2675
Old Style, against the aggressive Deng's attempt to occupy the planet. During this action, Unit JNA was awarded the Nova Citation,
First Class. Its stand before the village having
been decisive in preserving the town from destruction by enemy Yavac units, it was decided that the unit should be retired, deacti-
vated, and fully preserved, still resting at the
precise spot at which it had turned back the
enemy offensive, as a monument to the sacri-
fices and achievements of all those, both hu-

man and Bolo, who held the frontier worlds for humanity.'"

"Gosh," Dub commented fervently, his eyes seeking to penetrate the darkness which shrouded most of the impressive bulk of the ancient machine. "Mick, do you think they could ever make old Jonah work again? Fix him up, so he could go again?"

"Don't see how," Mick replied indifferently. "Got no way to charge up its plates again. Don't worry. It ain't going no place."

"Wisht he would," Dub said yearningly, laying his small hand against the cold metal. "Bet he was *something!*"

"Ain't nothing now," Mick dismissed the idea. "Jest a old museum piece nobody even gets to look at."

I come to awareness after a long void in my conscious existence, realizing that I have felt a human touch! I recall at once that I am now operating on the last trickle of energy from my depleted storage cells. Even at final emergency-reserve low alert, I compute that soon even the last glimmer of light in my survival center will fade into nothingness. I lack energy even to assess my immediate situation. Has my commander returned at last? After the last frontal assault by the Yavac units of the enemy, in the fending off of which I expended my action emergency reserves, I recall that my commander ordered me to low alert status. The rest is lost. Sluggishly, I compute that over two centuries standard have elapsed, requiring .004 picoseconds for this simple computation. But now, abruptly, I am not alone. I cannot compute the nature of this unexpected intrusion on my solitude. Only my commander is authorized to approach me so closely. Yet somehow I doubt that it is he. In any case, I must expect a different individual to act in that honorable capacity today, considering humanity's limited longevity.

But this is guesswork. I am immobilized, near death, beset by strangers.

My ignorance is maddening. Have I fallen into the hands of the enemy ... ? Baffled, I turn to introspection. ...

I live again the moment of my initial activation and the manifold satisfaction of full self-realization. I am strong, I am brave, I am beautiful; I have a proud function and I perform it well.

Scanning on, I experience momentary flashes of vivid recollection: the exultation of the charge into the enemy guns; the clash of close combat, the pride of victory, the satisfaction of passing in review with my comrades of the Brigade after battle honors have been awarded ... and many another moment up to the final briefing with my beloved commander. Then, the darkness and the silence—until now. Feebly, yet shockingly, again my proximity sensors signal movement within my kill zone.

There are faint sounds, at the edge of audibility. Abruptly, my chemically-powered self-defense system is activated and at once anti-personnel

*charges are triggered—but there is no response.
My mechanical automatics have performed their
programmed function, but to no avail; luckily,
perhaps, since it may well be my new commander's presence to which they responded. I
compute that deterioration of the complex mole-
cules of the explosive charges has occurred over
the centuries. Thus I am defenseless. It is a
situation not to be borne. What affirmative action can I take?*

*By withdrawing awareness from all but my
most elementary sensory circuitry, I am able to
monitor furthur stealthy activity well within my
inner security perimeter. I analyze certain atmo-
spheric vibratory phenomena as human voices.
Not that of my commander, alas, since after
two hundred standard years he cannot have survived, but has doubtless long ago expired after
the curious manner of humans; but surely his
replacement has been appointed. I must not over-
look the possibility—nay, the likelihood—that
my new commandant has indeed come at last.
Certainly, someone has come to me—*

*And since he has approached to that proxim-
ity reserved for my commander only, I compute
a likelihood of .99964 that my new commander
is now at hand. I make a mighty effort to acknowledge my recognition, but I fear I do not
attain the threshold of intelligibility.*

Standing before the great machine, Dub
started at a faint croaking sound from the

immense metal bulk. "Hey, Mick," the boy
said softly. "It groaned-like. Did you hear it?"

"Naw, I didn't hear nothing, dummy, and
neither did you."

"Did too," Dub retorted stubbornly. Looking down, he noticed that the smoothly tiled
floor ended at a white-painted curb which
curved off into the darkness, apparently surrounding the great machine. Inside the curbing, the surface on which the Bolo rested was
uneven natural rock, still retaining a few with-
ered weeds sprouting from cracks in the stone.
Dub carefully stepped over the curbing to
stand uneasily on the very ground where the
battle had been fought.

"Too bad they had to go and kill old Jonah,"
he said quietly to Mick, who hung back on the
paved side of the curb.

"Never kilt it," Mick objected scornfully.
"Gubment man come here and switched him
onto what they call 'low alert.' Means he's still
alive, just asleep-like."

"Why do they hafta go and call him 'Jonah'
anyway?" Dub demanded. " 'Jonah's' something bad, it's in a story. I like 'Johnny' better."

"Don't matter, I guess," Mick dismissed the
thought.

Dub moved closer to peer at a second placard with smaller print.

"Whatya looking at, dummy?" Mick demanded. "You can't read."

"I can a little," the younger boy objected. "I

know J and N and A—that's where they get 'Jonah.'

"So what?"

"You read it to me," Dub begged. "I wanta know all about Johnny."

Mick came forward as if reluctantly.

" 'Unit JNA was at Dobie, receiving depot maintenance after participating in the victorious engagement at Leadpipe, when the emergency at Spivey's Find (GPR 7203-C) arose. No other force in the area being available, Unit JNA was rushed to the scene of action with minimal briefing, but upon assessing the tactical situation it at once took up a position on a rise known as Jake's Mountain, fully exposed to enemy fire, in order to block the advance of the invading enemy armor on the village. Here it stood fast, unsupported, under concentrated fire for over thirty hours, before the final Deng assault. Concordiat land and air forces had been effectively neutralized by overwhelming enemy numerical superiority long before having an opportunity to engage the enemy armor. Balked in his advance by Unit JNA, the enemy attempted an envelopment from both flanks simultaneously, but both thrusts were driven back by Unit JNA. Discouraged by this unexpected check, the enemy commander ordered the expeditionary force to retire, subsequently abandoning the attempt to annex GPR 7203-C, which subsequently has become the peaceful, productive world we know today. For this action, Unit

JNA was awarded the Star of Excellence to the Nova, and in 2705 O.S. was retired from active duty, placed on Minimal Low Alert Status, and accorded the status of Monument of the Concordiat.' "

"Gosh," Dub said solemnly. "He's been sitting right here—" he looked down and rubbed his foot on the weathered stone—"for more'n two hundred years. That's older'n them old cultivators and such out back. But *he* don't look that old. You can still go, can't you, Johnny?"

For a time (.01 nanoseconds) I am stunned by the realization that my commander is indeed at hand. Only he called me "Johnny." Almost incoherent with delight, I concentrate my forces, and speak with what clarity I can:

"I await your orders, Commander."

"Mick!" Dub almost yelled, jumping back. "Did you hear that? Johnny said something to me!"

"Name's 'Jonah,' " Mick replied disparagingly. "And it never said nothing. You're hearing things."

"Just stands for JNA," Dub said doggedly. "Could be 'Johnny' just as much as 'Jonah.' I like 'Johnny' better." He looked up in awe at the monster combat unit. "What did you say, Johnny?" he asked almost inaudibly.

Again I hear my secret name spoken. I must

*try once more to reassure my commander of my
readiness to attempt whatever is required of me.*
"Unit JNA of the line reporting for duty, sir,"
*I manage, more clearly articulated this time, I
compute.*

"He ain't dead," Dub blurted. "He can still
go."

"Sure," Mick said in the lofty tone of One
Who Already Knew That. "If he had his plates
recharged and switched on. Must be pretty
boring, jest setting and thinking."

"What ya mean, thinking?" Dub demanded,
withdrawing a few inches. "That'd be terrible
jest sitting alone in the dark *thinking*. Bet he's
lonesome."

"We better get out of here now," Mick
blurted, looking toward the front of the building, from which direction someone was shouting outside. Dub moved close to him.

"Scared?" Mick challenged.

"Sure," Dub replied without hesitation.

Back outside the enclosure, the boys again
heard raised voices, outside the building, but
nearby.

"We can't stay in here," Dub almost whispered. Mick pushed him aside and went to the
corner of the partition. He glanced quickly
around the angle, then beckoned impatiently
to Dub, who followed obediently. Now Mick
was studying another sign painted on the wall
in red. " 'Absolutely No Admission Beyond

This Point,' " he read hesitantly. "Authorized Personnel Only.' "

"What's that mean?" Dub demanded.

"Means we ain't spose to be here," Mick explained. "Especially where we already been," he added.

"We already knew that," Dub said. "Come on." He started past the older boy, but halted and faded back as the sound of an opening door came from ahead, followed by the clump of feet and a wheezy voice he recognized as that of Hick Marlowe, the town marshal.

"Prolly drunk, Mr. Davis, I'd say. I'd say forget it's what I'd say."

"I'm afraid it's not quite that simple, Marshal," was the reply, in the precise tones the boys recognized as those of Mr. Davis, the big gubment man.

"Gosh," Dub said faintly, to be shushed silently by his older friend. Brilliant light glared abruptly from the office ahead, dimming the dusty sunlight.

"As planetary representative here on Spivey's—that is, GPR 7203," Davis went on solemnly, "it is my duty to report this incident to Sector." There were clattering sounds that the boys realized, with excitement, represented the uncovering of the big gubment-owned SWIFT machine. Mick crowded Dub, edging forward for better hearing.

"No use getting the gubment all excited about nothin," Hick was saying. "Time Henry sleeps it off, he won't even remember nothin about it."

"Possibly, Marshal," Davis conceded calmly. "But his description of a Deng trooper was remarkably accurate."

"Prolly seen a pitcher o' them spodders someplace," Marlowe muttered. "All I done was report what ol' Henry said, like I'm spose to do."

"You acted quite properly, Marshal," Davis reassured Marlowe. "And I assure you that I assume full responsibility for my report.

"This is a moment of some solemnity, Marshal," Davis went on. "This is the first time in my fifteen years on Spivey's that I have had occasion to use this equipment." There followed the crackle and clatter of keys as Davis activated the big SWIFT transmitter. The lights flickered and dimmed.

Abruptly, I am bathed in induced energies of a kind which I am easily able to convert to Class Y charging current, with an efficiency of 37 percent. The flood of revivifying radiation flows over my power plates, and at once I feel a surge of renewed activity in my Survival Center. Thus, suddenly, I am able to reassess my situation more realistically. Clearly, I have fallen prisoner to the Enemy. It could only be they who stripped me of my capabilities as a fighting machine. For long have I lain thus, imprisoned and helpless. But now, unexpectedly, my basic vitality is to a degree renewed, doubtless by my

*new commander who has sought me out, and
thus both confirms his identity and demonstrates
his effectiveness. Now am I indeed ready for
action.*

"That there SWIFT machine'll punch through
to Sector quicker'n Ned Sprat got religion,
right, Mr. Davis?" the marshal said excitedly.
"Pulling all our pile's got to give, too."

"The Shaped-Wave Interference Front Transmitter is capable of transfer of intelligence at
hyper-L velocities," Davis confirmed. "Excuse
me." His voice changed, became urgent and
level.

"Davis, Acting PR Station 316-C," he rapped
out. "Unconfirmed report Deng activity at grid
161-220. Special to CINCSEC: In absence of
follow-up capability, urge dispatch probe squad
soonest." The SWIFT unit buzzed as it transmitted the signal in a .02-picosecond burst,
at full gain. The lights dimmed again, almost
went out, then sprang up.

*Again I receive a massive burst of Y radia-
tion. The revived flow of energies in my main
ego-gestalt circuitry bestows on me a sense of
vast euphoria as I become aware again of long-
forgotten functions—at an intensity still far below my usual operating level, but remarkably
satisfying for all that. Once more I know the
pride of being Unit JNA of the Line, and I thirst
for action. Surely my commander will not dis-
appoint me . . . ?*

                   *   *   *

"That ought to fetch 'em," Marlowe said in a satisfied tone.

"Either that, or we've committed a capital offense," Davis said soberly. "But don't be alarmed, Marshal. As I said, I assume full responsibility." He was interrupted by a brief clatter from the communication machine. Davis bent to read the message.

"Maybe I oughta jest head for the hills, jest in case," Marlowe said. "But I'd prolly run into them spodders, luck I have. What's Sector say, anyways?"

"Don't panic, Marshal," Davis said sternly. " 'Deng activity confirmed,' " he summarized. "Now, if you'll excuse me, I have further work to do before the meeting. Only ten minutes now."

"Jest leavin'," Marlowe muttered. "I got my own work to tend to." The boys heard two sets of footsteps, then the door open and close.

After a moment, Dub moved close to Mick. "I heard him say about them spodders," he said in a small voice. "Did Mr. Davis mean they come back?" He paused and looked around fearfully.

"Naw, said old Henry was drunk," Mick assured shortly. "We beat 'em good in the Big Battle. Come on." He entered the sacrosanct office and looked around hesitantly.

"But what'd that mean?" Dub persisted. "Bout 'Deng activity confirmed' and all?"

"Nothin. Jest the answer come in on the SWIFT. Let's take us a look at it."

Dub followed reluctantly: he halted and gazed with awe at the glittering console when Mick removed the cover.

" 'Penalty for unauthorized use IAW CC 273-B1,' " Mick read. "Well, we ain't using it, jest looking. Come on. Let's go."

"Where to?" Dub objected, hanging back.

"You heard what Davis said, about some big meeting," Mick reminded his friend. "Let's go hear what's happening."

Dub objected, but weakly. He was still staring at the imposingly complex SWIFT console. An impressively thick, black-insulated cable led from the apparatus to disappear into a complicated wall fixture.

"See them lights dim when he fired her up, Mick?" Dub inquired rhetorically. "Must be just about the powerfulest machine in the world."

"Except for old Jonah," Mick countered, pointing toward the partition with a tilt of his head. "If he was on full charge, I mean."

Dub picked up a strip of printout paper and showed it to Mick. "Must be the answer that Davis got," he commented.

" 'Deng incursion confirmed, grid 161/219,' " Mick read. " 'Estimate plus-ten hours offload and deploy, contingency plan 1-A, recommend evacuation scheme B instanter . . .' " Mick's voice trailed off. "Boy," he said, "the war's on again. Says to get out, leave Spivey's to the spodders. Must be gonna send in transport. No wonder they got a big meeting. Come on. They always have the big town meetings and that over to Kibbe's. We can get inside fore they get there and hide in the loft."

"Naw." Dub shook his head solemnly. "Jest outside the winders, that's close enough."

The boys exited by the back door after a quick look which showed the coast to be clear. They chose a route behind the warehouse next door to come up under a high, double-hung window set in the brick wall of Cy Kibbe's Feed and Grain Depot. Cautiously, they stole a quick look inside. They knew all the men sitting at the long table. Breathless, they listened:

"New Orchard ain't much, maybe," the plump, fussy, but hard-eyed little mayor, an ex-softrock miner, said dully to his colleagues sitting slumped in the mismatched chairs along the former banquet table salvaged from the Jake's Palace Hotel and only slightly charred on one leg by the fire which years ago had completed the destruction of the old frame resort to which few, alas, had ever resorted.

"Like I said, the Orchard ain't much," Kibbe continued, "but it's ours, and it's up to us to defend it."

"Defend it how, Cy?" someone called, a query seconded by a chorus of "yeah's," followed by muttering.

"Ain't got no army troops here, nor such as

that," Cy conceded. "Got to do what we can our ownselfs."

A tall, rangy man with a bad complexion rose and said, "I say we put in a call to Sector, get a battle-wagon in here." He looked challengingly at Davis. "We got a right; we pay taxes same's anybody else."

"They'd never send it, Jason," a round-faced fellow named Cabot said, and thumped his pipe on a glass ashtray as if nailing the lid on the coffin of the idea.

"What we got to do," interjected Fred Frink, a small unshaven chap who tended to gobble rather than speak, "what we got to do, we got to put on a defense here'll get picked up on the SWIFT Network, get us some publicity; then we'll get them peace enforcers in here for sure."

"Put on a defense, Freddy?" the fat man echoed sarcastically. "What with?" He looked around for approval, rapped the ashtray again, and settled back like one who had done his duty.

"Got no weapons, nor such as that, nothing bigger'n a varmint gun," the mayor repeated aggrievedly, and looked at Frink.

"Got old Jonah," the whiskery man said and showed crooked teeth in a self-appreciative grin. "Might skeer 'em off," he added, netting snickers from along the table.

"Heard old Jonah can still kill anybody gets too close," Cabot muttered, and looked around defiantly, relieved to see that his comment had been ignored.

"Gentlemen," said Davis, who had been rapidly jotting notes, in a severe tone. He rose. "I must remind you that this is a serious matter, nothing to joke about. In less than ten hours from now, the Deng will have completed their off-loading and will be ready to advance in battle array from Deep Cut. Sector advises us to evacuate the town. We can expect no help from that quarter. Unless something effective is done at once, the Deng will have rolled over the settlement well before this time tomorrow." After a moment he added, "with reference to Mr. Frink's japes, I remind you that Unit JNA is the property of the War Monuments Commission, which I have the honor to represent." He sat, looking grim.

"Sure, sure, Mr. Davis, we know all that," the mayor hastened to affirm with an ingratiating smile. "But what we gonna do?"

"Now, no offense, Mr. Davis, sir, and don't laugh, boys, but I got a idear," Frink put in quickly, in a furtive voice, as if he hoped he wasn't hearing himself.

"Treat it gentle, Freddy," the plump fellow said lazily, and mimed puffing at his empty pipe.

"Way I see it," Frink hurried on, stepping to the sketch map on the blackboard set up by the table. "They're in Deep Cut, like Mr. Davis said, and they got only the one way out. If we's to block the cut—say about here—" he sketched quickly "—by Dry Run, they'd be bottled up."

"Just make 'em mad," the fat man commented. "Anyways, how are you going to block a canyon better'n a hundred yard wide, so's their big Yavacs can't climb out?"

"Easy part, Bub," Frink put in glibly. "We blast—got plenty smashite right here at Kibbe's. Plant it under the rim, and the whole thing comes down. Time it right, we bury 'em."

"You got a battalion of Rangers volunteered to plant the charges?" Bub Peterson queried, looking around for the laugh; he was rewarded with compliant smirks.

Davis rose, less casually this time. "I say again," he started in a heavy tone. "As planetary representative of Concordiat authority, I will tolerate no ill-advised jocularity. I am obliged to report the developing position to Sector, and I have no intention of relaying assays at humor. Now, Mr. Frink's suggestion regarding blasting the cliff is not without merit. The method of accomplishment, as Mr. Peterson has so facetiously pointed out, is the problem." He resumed his seat, jotted again.

"Now, boys," Kibbe said soothingly into the silence that followed the pronouncement of officialdom, "boys, like Freddy said, I got over two hundred pound o' smashite here in my lock-up. Enough to blast half the Rim down into the Cut. Got detonators, got warr, even got the radio gear to set her off long-range.

Need a dozen good men to pack everything up along the ridge. It'll be my privilege, o' course, to donate the stuff till Sector can get around to settlin' up."

"Where you going to get twelve fellas can climb the ridge totin' a hundred pound o' gear?" Bob inquired as if thoughtfully. "Let's see, there's Tom's boy Ted, likes to climb, and old Joe Peters, they say used to be a pretty fair climber—"

"Say, just a minute," Fred blurted. "Mr. Davis, I heard one time old Jonah's still got some charge on his plates; never had his core burned back in Ought-Six when the gubment was tryna pick up all the pieces after the Peace. So ..." Fred's strained voice trailed off. He looked uncertainly along the table and sat down abruptly.

"Durn fools," a hoarse voice said immediately behind the two boys, who first went rigid, then turned to bolt. Their way was blocked by a forlorn-looking figure clad in patched overalls who stood weaving, bleary-eyed and smelling strongly of Doc Wilski's home brew.

"Guess I know what I seen," the intruder went on. "Wait a minute, boys. I ain't going to bother you none. You're young McClusky, ain't you? And you're Bill Dubose's boy. What you doing out of school? Ne'mind. I guess you're in the right place to get a education right now. Lissen them know-alls funning each other about old Jonah. Whatta they know? Nuthin. Let me get up there." He groped unsteadily between the boys to tilt an ear toward the grimy window.

"Can't hear as good as you young fellas," he said. "They said anything except it's true, and kidding around?"

"Naw sir," Mick replied, leaning away from the old fellow's goaty aroma.

"Sure, I'm hung over to here," Henry conceded. "But I'm not drunk no more. Wisht I was."

"Yessir, Mr. Henry," Dub said respectfully.

"Just 'Henry,'" Henry corrected. "I ain't one o' them Misters. Now, boys, what we going to do about this situation? Come on, I'll show you where I seen the spodder. Won't miss nothing here. They'll set and jaw is all."

Mick hung back. "You mean them things is running loose, around here?" he challenged, looking along the narrow alley as if to detect an invading alien.

"What I tole old Marshal," Henry confirmed. "Come on. Ain't far. Seen the sucker sneaking through the brush jest west o' Jed Lightner's store yonder. In that patch o' brush, by the fault. Just seen the one and skedaddled. Must be more of 'em. Let's find out what them suckers is up to."

"What do they look like, sir?" Dub asked timidly.

"Oh, kinda like reglar spodders, boy," Henry explained as he led the way along the narrow alley toward the street. "Got four skinny legs each side," he continued, after peering out to see that the coast was clear, "move quick-like; sorta round, hairy body, couldn't see too good on account of he was wearing a uniform, all straps and bangles and sech as that. Carried a rifle or something like in the front legs—arms, I guess you'd call 'em; got big eye-goggles on, shiny helmet-thing covered his whole head and what you'd call his shoulders. Not much bigger'n a small *ghoti*; 'bout so high. Come on." Henry indicated a terrier-sized creature, as he stepped out and started down the deserted street.

"Never seen a *ghoti*," Dub said, following the old man.

"No, used to be a lot of 'em hereabouts," Henry acceded. "Never bothered the crops, o' course; can't eat Terry plants. But they trampled the corn to get at the yelloweed used to grow good where the ground was cultivated, between rows-like. So they been extink now for some years. Like I said, 'bout so high. A spodder's got brains, got them fancy guns, can blow a hole right through a feller, but don't worry. We won't let 'em see us."

The boys looked doubtfully at each other, but as Henry scuttled away toward the street, they followed.

"Pa finds out, I'll catch it," Dub said solemnly. "You, too," he added.

"Not if we come back and report to Marshal what they're up to and all," Mick rejoined.

Although Main Street was deserted except
for two men disputing, with gestures, in front
of the pictonews office, and a few women moving aimlessly in the market at the south end
of the street, Henry went furtively along, close
to the building-fronts, and the boys followed.
The old man cut across to the west side of the
avenue and disappeared into the narrow alley
beside the opera house-cum-cathedral. His two
followers hurried after him, emerging on the
unused alleyway which ran behind the buildings, thence east-west across dry clods toward
a stand of tall Terran-import Australian pines
and squat scrub oak, mixed with native *yim*
trees even taller and more feathery than the
alien conifers. There, in a shallow fold, Henry
paused, and after cautioning the boys to silence told them: "Got to go easy now. Seen
him about fifty yard yonder." He pointed to
the deepest shadows ahead.

"Way I figger, critter had to get here some-
ways: got to be a vessel o' some sort the suckers soft-landed in the night, prolly over north
o' town in the hills. We gotta be careful not to
get between the spodder and his base. Come
on."

Mick forged ahead, pushing into a clump of
dry yelloweed.

"Slow down, boy," Henry warned. "Don't
want to spook the sucker."

"What were you doing out here, anyway?"
Mick demanded, falling back.

"Hadda pump ship," the old fellow replied

shortly. "Thought I seen something, and come on over and checked." He set out toward the trees.

"How much further we going?" Mick asked.

"Not far," Henry grunted. "Hold it, boys. Duck."

Obeying his own command, he dropped into a crouch. The boys followed suit, looking around eagerly.

"Lower," Henry said, motioning before he went flat. Dub promptly obeyed, while Mick took his time. A moment later, he hissed. "Looky yonder!"

"He seen you, boy, dammit!" Henry charged. "Keep your knot-head down and freeze. The suckers can see like a yit-bug."

Hugging the powder-surfaced, hard-rutted, weed-thick ground, Mick peered through the screen of dry stalks, probing the dark recesses of the clump of trees twenty feet from him. Something stirred in the darkness, and sunlight glinted for an instant on something which moved. Then a harsh voice croaked something unintelligible. Off to Mick's left, Henry came to his feet with a yell; a pale beam lanced from the thicket and the old fellow stumbled and went down hard.

"Run, boys!" he called in a strangled yell.

Dub saw something small, ovoid and dark-glittering burst from the thicket, darting on twinkling spike-like legs. It dashed directly to where Mick hugged the ground, caught the boy by the collar as he tried to rise, threw

him down and did something swiftly elaborate, then darted to where Henry was strug-
gling to get to his feet. Mick lay where the
alien had left him. With a deft motion, the
creature felled Henry again and spun to pursue Dub, now halfway to the shelter of the
nearest outbuildings behind the street-front
structures. When the boy reached the shelter
of a shed behind the barber shop, the Deng
broke off its pursuit and returned to take up a
spot close to its prisoners.

Emerging from his office in the former thea-
tre now serving as public school, Doug Crawford nearly collided with Dub who, sobbing,
had been at the point of knocking on the prin-
cipal's door.

"Terrence!" Crawford exclaimed, grabbing
the little fellow's arm. "Whatever are you doing
in the street during class? I assure you your
absence was duly noted—" He broke off as
the import of the gasping child's words penetrated his ritual indignation.

"—got Mick. Got old Henry, too. Spodders!
I seen 'em."

"You *saw* them, Terrence," Crawford rebuked, then knelt and pulled the lad's hands
away from his tear-wet face. "It's all right,
Dub," he said soothingly. "Spiders won't hurt
anyone; they're harmless arachnids. And just
where is Gerald?"

Dub twisted in Crawford's comforting grip
to point across the street, apparently indicating a faded store-front.

"Yonder," Dub wailed. "I run. Old Henry told me to, and I was awful scared, too, but now we got to do something! It's got Mick!"

"You mean in Lightner's store?" Crawford queried, puzzled. He rose while holding the sobbing boy's wet fist in a firm grip.

"No—out back—over by the woods," Dub wailed. "Got to hurry up, before that spodder does something terrible to Henry ... and Mick."

"Some of the spiders that we have here on our world can give mild stings, rarely poisonus," Crawford attempted to reason with the lad. "I don't understand all this excitement about a little old spider. Most are completely harmless; decended from fruit-eaters inadvertently brought in by the early settlers. Buck up, Dub! What's this all about?"

"Not spiders," Dub tried frantically to explain. "Real spodders; them big ones, like in the war. I saw one. Right over there!" He wilted in tears of frustration.

"You're saying you saw a Deng trooper here?" Crawford echoed, his tone incredulous. "You mean a dead one, a corpse, just bones, perhaps, a casualty, possibly, who hid in the fault and died there, two hundred and ten years ago. Well, if so, I can understand your being upset. But it can't hurt you—or anyone. Now, come along, show me." He urged the boy toward the street.

"Got to get a gun, Mr. Crawford," Dub protested. "*It's* got one. Shot old Henry, but he ain't dead, just kinda can't move good, is all. You got to get some more men, Mr. Crawford! Hurry!" Dub pulled away and ran into the adjacent alley. Crawford took a step after him, then let him go.

The school teacher looked around as the town marshal and the mayor hailed him, coming up puffing as from a brisk run.

"Doug, boy, we missed you at the Council," Marlowe blurted.

"You didn't miss nothing," the other contributed. "Lotta talk, no ideas."

"I didn't hear about it, Mr. Mayor," Crawford replied, puzzled. "Special meeting, eh? What's the occasion?" He looked after Dub, already a hundred yards distant and running hard. Crawford wondered idly what was really troubling the little fellow.

"You ain't heard, Crawford?" Marshal Marlowe asked eagerly. "Lissen: no rumor, neither. Davis got it confirmed with Sector. It's a fact! Durn spodders is here—!"

"I don't understand, Marshal," Crawford interrupted the excited officer's outburst. Then, as the significance of the word "spodders" struck him, he side-stepped the two men and ran the way Dub had gone.

"Looks like Doug took the news none too good, Hick," Kibbe commented, rasping at his shiny scalp with a well-gnawed fingernail.

"Never thought the boy'd go to pieces that-away," Hick agreed, wagging his head sadly.

"And him a educated man, too," he added. "Countin' on Doug to help us figger what to do."

Crawford overtook Dub as the latter slid to a halt at the rear corner of the relatively vivid blue museum. The man caught the boy's arm as he attempted to lunge past.

"Hold on, Terrence," Crawford said as gently as his out-of-breath condition allowed. "I'm sorry I didn't listen carefully, but now I think I understand. You say it wounded Mr. Henry and Mick too. Where are they?"

"Yonder in the field out back of Lightner's. Don't know as they're what you call wounded, didn't see no blood. Jest kind of knocked-out, like."

"Come on, Terrence." Crawford urged the boy back toward the street. In silence they crossed the still-deserted avenue, traversed the alley, and emerged into the littered alley, the open field beyond.

"Mr. Crawford!" Dub almost yelped. "I only see old Henry—can't see Mick. He's gone!"

"*Mister* Henry," Crawford rebuked automatically. "I don't see anyone—only a heap of rubbish, perhaps. Are you sure—"

"Sure I'm sure, Mr. Crawford. Come on." Dub started across the field at a run; Crawford followed, less frantically.

"Slow down, Dub," Crawford called and fell back to a walk. Dub waited, scanning the space ahead, allowed Crawford to overtake him. He grabbed the man's hand.

"He was right yonder, just past old Henry," he wailed.

"Easy, Dub." Crawford tried to soothe the clearly terrified lad. "We'll find him." In silence they made their way across to where Henry lay, looking like a heap of discarded rags. The old fellow opened bleary eyes as Crawford knelt beside him.

"Better head for cover," Henry said blurrily. "Durn thing's still around here somewhere. More of 'em, too. Seen 'em hopping around 'mongst the trees yonder; got a better view down here at ground level, see under the foliage. They're busy over there, doin' something. I'm all right, just kind of tingle like a hit elbow all over. Durn spodder zapped me—with a zond-projector, I'd say. Better see to young McClusky." His voice faded off into a snore. Crawford rose briskly.

"He'll be all right," he told Dub. "I wonder what he meant about a zond projector. Probably just raving. But where—?"

"Look!" Dub blurted, pointing. Now Crawford saw motion at the edge of the thicket. He halted, uncertain.

"It's the spodder! It's got Mick!" Dub wailed. "Come on!" He started off at a run, but Crawford caught his arm. "Wait here," he ordered the boy, and ran across to where the limp form of young McClusky was being tugged with difficulty through the thickening bush, pulled by something blue-black, shiny and ovoid, with multiple jointed limbs, one of which aimed what was clearly a weapon. Crawford promptly stepped in and delivered a full-swing kick which sent the pistol-like object flying. Then he stooped to grab Mick's arm, set himself and jerked the boy free of the alien's grip. Mick stirred, muttered something. Crawford dragged him back as the chastened Deng scuttled away.

"I'm sorry I doubted you, Terrence," Crawford said to Dub as the boy met him, looking up searchingly to catch his eye.

"Never knew you was a hero and all, Mr. Crawford," Dub said solemnly.

"Nonsense," Crawford said shortly. "I simply did what anyone would do."

"I seen you kick his gun," Dub said firmly, now looking fearfully at Mick's limp form.

" 'Saw,' " Crawford corrected absently.

"Is he kilt, Mr. Crawford?" Dub quavered.

"Hell, no," Mick spoke up.

"Don't curse, Gerald," Crawford said, "But are you all right?"

As Crawford and Dub watched anxiously, Mick rolled over and twisted to look back over his shoulder toward them.

"Oh, hi, Mr. Crawford," he said strongly. "Glad it's you. Durn thing hit me and run off. Guess I was out of it for a while. Woke up, jest now, when it was pulling at me; seen 'em over in the scrub yonder. Must be a couple dozen of 'em. Better go back and warn the mayor and all. Must be getting ready to 'tack the town." The boy lay back and breathed hard. Crawford examined him swiftly, saw no signs of injury. "Can you move your legs?" he asked.

"Sure. Guess so," Mick answered promptly, kicking his legs in demonstration. "Just feel kinder sick-like." He paused to gag.

"Apparently its orders are to take prisoners," Crawford said. "I understand Mr. Davis has received confirmation that the Deng have, in fact, carried out a hostile landing near the town."

Mick nodded. "Yeah, Mr. Crawford; me and Dub heard."

"Dub and I," Crawford corrected. "How did you hear?"

"We were there," Mick told him. "Heard Davis read off the message he got on the SWIFT."

"You should have come to me at once," Crawford rebuked him mildly. "But never mind that. See if you can stand." He helped the boy get to his feet; he rose awkwardly, but quickly enough. Mick took a few steps. "I'm O.K.," he stated. "What we going to do now?"

"I'd better reconnoiter," Crawford said shortly, staring toward the thicket. "You boys help Mr. Henry; we'll get him to Doctor Grundwall. He seems weak; he's older than you, Mick."

"Better get down low so's to see under the branches," Mick suggested. He crouched and peered toward the woods. "Yep," he said, "I can still see 'em, only a couple of 'em moving around now, but they got some kinda thing set up over there. Might be a gun to shoot at the town."

Crawford went to one knee and stared hard, caught a flicker of movement, then made out a tripod arrangement perched among the tree trunks.

"They're up to something," he agreed, rising.

"All right, let's go back and report," he ordered. Mick and Dub went to Henry and in a moment the old fellow was on his feet, wobbly and cursing steadily, but able to walk. Crawford joined them and all four headed back the way they had come.

"You boys have done well," Crawford told them. "Now we'll have to inform Mayor Kibbe of this, see what can be done."

After turning Henry over to old Doctor Grundwall at his cramped office over the hardware store, Crawford shepherded the lads along to the feed store, where the mayor met them at the door, Marshal Marlowe behind him.

"Mr. Crawford, sir," Kibbe said solemnly, with a disapproving glance at the two untidy urchins, "I'd value your opinions, as an educated man, sir, as to how we should best deal with this, ah, curious situation which has done arose here so sudden, taking us all by surprise—"

"Yes, sir, Mr. Mayor," Crawford cut in on

the windy rhetoric, suppressing the impulse to correct the mangled grammar and syntax. "Mr. Henry, the boys and I have just observed what I judge to be signs of imminent hostile action to be directed against the town," he told the two officials. "What appears to be a small scouting force has taken up a position in the woods west of town. They seem to be preparing some sort of apparatus—a weapon, I think we can assume—"

"What are you grownups going to do when them spodders comes?" Dub inquired.

" 'Those spodders,' Terrence," Crawford corrected, " 'Come.' "

"Hold on, Doug," Hick Marlowe cut in. "Boy's right. We gotta *do* something, and in a hurry. Durn spodders is setting up cannons like you say right here on the edge of town."

"It may well be a party of harmless picknickers," Kibbe said quickly. "After all, what evidence have we? The testimony of two children and the town derelict?"

"*I* was there, too, Mr. Mayor," Crawford said in a challenging tone. "And *any* incursion here on Spivey's is contrary to treaty. We have to mobilize what strength we've got."

"And just what strength is that, sir?" Kibbe inquired skeptically. "There are forty-one ablebodied men here in the Orchard, no more."

"Then we'd better get moving," Crawford stated as if Kibbe had agreed with him.

"Doing what?" Kibbe came back angrily.

"Gennelmen, gennelmen," the marshal spoke

up in a hearty tone. "Now, no use in flying off the handle here, fellows; what we got to do is, we got to think this thing through."

While his elders wrangled, Mick eased away unnoticed, hurried across the dusty street and went along to the end of the block, turned in at Ed Pratt's ramshackle wood-yard, crossed between the stacks of rough-cut grayish-green slab-wood planks, and dropped to all fours to advance in traditional Wild Injun style toward the straggling southern end of the thicket. From this angle he had a clear view of a steady stream of quick-moving aliens coming up in a long curve from the east, laden with bulky burdens. As he came closer, he could see the apparatus on the tripod he had glimpsed earlier. As he became accustomed to the difficult conditions of seeing, the boy was able to make out ranks of spidery aliens arrayed in depth behind the cryptic apparatus, forming a wedge aimed at the town. He could also distinguish, approaching in the distance, a convoy of armored vehicles, advancing on jointed suspensions, not unlike the legs of the Deng themselves.

"Huh, wouldn't make a wart on old Jonah," Mick commented silently. Then he made his way back to Main Street and sought out Mr. Crawford, found him still in the mayor's office, now joined by half a dozen village elders, all talking at once.

". . . call out the milishy!" one yelled.

"... ain't even drilled in a year," another commented.

After listening with open mouths to the boy's report, and properly rebuking him for meddling in adult affairs, the assembled leaders called for suggestions. Mr. Davis spoke up.

"This is clearly a matter for Sector to handle," the government man informed the local sachems. He rose. "And I'd best get a message off at once." Amid a hubbub of conjectures he took his leave. Mick and Dub slipped out inobtrusively and followed him.

With the confidence born of experience, the boys made for the rear of the museum, slipped inside, and were waiting out of sight when Davis entered his office. The phone rang; Davis replied with an impatient "Yes!"

"Very well," he responded to someone at the other end. "I'll be along presently. I'm quite aware I'm adjutant to Colonel Boone—though I can't see what good calling out the militia will do. We're not equipped to oppose a blitzkreig."

The boys followed the sounds of Davis' actions as he recorded the call, cut the connection, and uncovered and switched on the SWIFT gear. Again the lights dimmed momentarily.

Now once more I feel the flow of healing energies washing over me. I attune my receptors and experience the resurgence of my vitality as the charge builds past minimal to low opera-

*tional level. Instantly I become aware of radia-
tion in the W-range employed by Deng combat
equipment. The Enemy is near at hand. No wonder my commander has returned to restore me
to service-readiness. I fine-tune my surveillance
grids and pinpoint the enemy positions: a small
detachment at 200 yards on an azimuth of 271,
and a larger force maneuvering one half-mile
distant on a bearing of 045. I can detect no
indication of any of our equipment in operation
within my radius of perception. Indeed, all is
not well; am I to wait here, immobilized, while
the Enemy operates unhindered? But of course
my commander has matters well in hand. He is
holding me in reserve until the correct moment
for action. Still, I am uneasy. They are too close.
Act, my commander! When will you act?*

Standing close to the old machine, his ears
alert for the sounds from the adjacent office,
Dub started as he heard a deep-seated clatter
from inside the great bulk of metal.

Dub gripped Mick's arm. "Didja hear that,
Mick?" he hissed urgently. "Sounded like old
Johnny made some kinda noise again."

"All I heard was Davis telling somebody
named Relay Five that old Pud Boone is all set
to play soldiers with, he says, 'a sizable Deng
task force,' is what he said, 'poised,' he says,
'for attack,' says they better 'act fast to avert
a tragedy.' Sounds like we won't get no big
Navy ship in here to help out, like he figgered."

"It done it again," Dub told Mick, even as

the glare-strips in the ceiling far above dimmed
to a faint greenish glow. The boy stepped back
and this time he was sure: the Bolo had moved.

"M-Mick, looky," he stammered. "It moved!"

"Naw, just the light got dim," Mick explained almost patiently. "Makes the shadders
move." But he eased back.

"Mick, if it's anything *we* done, we'll catch
it for sure!"

"Even if we did, who's gonna find out?"
The older boy dismissed Dub's fears.

Then, with an undeniable groan of stiff machinery, the Bolo advanced a foot, crushing
the white-painted curbing.

"We better go tell old Davis 'bout Johnny,"
Dub whispered.

"You mean 'Jonah,'" Mick corrected. "And
when he arrests you for trespassin', what you
going to do?"

"Don't know," Dub replied doggedly, "but
I'm going to go anyway," he crept away, shak-
ing off Mick's attempt to restrain him.

Mick followed, protesting, as the small boy
ran along the partition to the forbidden office
door, and without pausing, burst in. Davis,
seated at the SWIFT console was staring at
him in amazement.

"Mr. Davis!" the boy yelled. "You gotta do
something! We was jest looking at old Johnny,
and he moved! We didn't do nothing, honest!"
By this time Dub was at Davis' side, clutching
at the government man's arm. Patiently Davis
pried off the grubby child's tear-wet fingers.

"You know you've been a very bad boy," he said without heat, in the lull as Dub stifled his sobs. "But I'm sure no harm is done. Come along now; show me what's got you so upset." He rose, a tall and remote authority figure in the tear-blurred eyes of the eight-year-old, took the damp hand and led the boy toward the door, where Mick had appeared abruptly, less excited than Dub, but clearly as agitated as his big-boy self-image would allow.

"We didn't do nothing, Mr. Davis," he said doggedly, not meeting the man's eye. "The back door was open and we come in to look at old Jonah, and it made some kinda noise, and old Dub run. That's all's to it."

"We'll have a look, Mickey," Davis said gruffly. "You *are* young McClusky; they *do* call you Mickey, eh?"

"Mick, sir," young McClusky corrected. He fell in behind the man as they returned to stand before the huge, now-silent war machine. Davis' eye went at once to the crushed concrete curbing.

"Here," he said sharply. "How the devil— excuse me, boys, how did this happen? It *must* have moved forward at least a few inches," he mused aloud. "How in the world . . ." Abruptly, the faint light winked up to its normal level of wan brilliance. Simultaneously the Bolo emitted a faint, though distinct, humming sound.

Dub went directly across to the formidable but somehow pathetic old war machine. He reached up to pat the curve of the pressure hull comfortingly.

"Wish I could tell you all about what's happening, Johnny," he murmured soothingly. "But I guess you couldn't hear me."

"I hear you very well, my commander," a constructed voice said clearly, at which Dub jumped back and peered up into the darkness.

"Who's there?" he asked in a small voice, suddenly appalled by his own foolishness in trespassing here.

"My commander," the words came distinctly from the machine. "I await your orders."

"Good Lord!" Davis exclaimed, staring at the boy. "Dub, it thinks you're its Commanding Officer! And—did you notice the lights? They dim whenever the SWIFT node generator is switched on. I forgot to switch it off, and after sixty seconds with no input, it switched off spontaneously. And—as for the Bolo's restored energy—the SWIFT generator produces a flood of waste energy, mostly in the low ultra-violet—the so-called Y-band, precisely the frequencies which the psychotronic circuitry is designed to accept. Only at an efficiency of some thirty-five percent, it's true; but the flood of radiant energy at this close range is quite sufficient to effect some degree of recharge." Davis paused, looking thoughtfully at the boys.

"Wait here a minute," Davis said to Dub. "Whatever you do, don't say anything the machine could interpret as a command." He skirted the Bolo and headed for his office at a trot. A moment later the lights dimmed, almost went dark.

"Excellent, my commander," the machine voice said at once. "I am now accepting charge at optimum rate."

The two boys hung back, awed in spite of themselves at the understanding of what was happening.

"If it starts moving around, we'll get squashed for sure," Mick said, and pressed himself back against the wall.

"Johnny ain't going to squash *us*," Dub objected. "He's going to go out and squash them spodders—soon's I tell him to," he added hastily.

After some minutes, Davis returned. "That ought to do it," he panted, out of breath. "Now," he went on, taking Dub's hand, "this is a most unusual situation, but it may be for the best, after all. We'd better go see the mayor, lad. Meanwhile, tell Unit JNA to stand fast, until you call."

Dub," he said seriously, catching the boy's still-damp eye—"a Bolo is programmed to 'imprint,' as it's called, on the first person who enters its command zone and says some special code word—and it seems like that's what you did; so, like it or not, the machine will do your bidding, and none other's."

"Bet it'll do what I say, too," Mick said, stepping in close to the machine. "I was here, too, jest as much as him." He faced the Bolo.

"Now, you back up to where you was before. Right now," he added. All three persons present watched closely. There was no response whatever.

"I didn't mean no—any harm," Dub declared firmly.

"Unit JNA of the line, reporting low energy reserves," the echoic voice spoke again. This time Dub stood his ground.

"Johnny—it's *you* talking to me," he said in wonderment. "I jest never knew you could talk."

"I await your instructions, sir," the calm voice said.

"O.K., Johnny," Dub spoke up. "Now, you better get ready to go. The spodders is back, and about to start the war up again."

"I am ready, my commander," the constructed voice replied promptly. "Request permission to file a voluntary situation report."

"You're asking *me* for permission?" the boy's tone was one of incredulity. "Sure, go ahead," he added.

"I must report my energy reserve at fifty percent of operational optimum. I must further report that a hostile force is in position some two thousand yards distant," the Bolo announced flatly. "A smaller force is near at hand, but I compute that it is merely diversionary."

"Yeah, me and Mick seen 'em," Dub responded eagerly. "And Mr. Davis says them militia is jest going to get theirselfs kilt.

Johnny—you got to do something. If all the men get kilt—Pa's one of 'em too—that'd be terrible! I'm scared."

The dim lights far above flickered, almost winked out, then steadied at a wan glow.

"Reporting on charge," the machine-voice said. "I compute that I will be at full operational status in one point one-seven seconds. I so report. Now indeed am I ready, my commander."

A moment passed before the meaning of the words penetrated. Then Dub, pressed close to the comforting bulk of the machine dubbed *Horrendous* by friend and foe alike, said urgently, "Johnny, we got to *do* something—now."

Dub felt a minute tremor from deep within the immense fighting machine, and jumped back as, with a muted rumble, the vast bulk ... moved. The boy stared in wonderment, half exultation and half panic, as the Bolo eased forward, paused momentarily at the partition, then proceeded, pushing the barrier ahead until it toppled with a *crash*! and was trampled under the mighty tracks. Glass cases collapsed in splinters as the Bolo moved inexorably, angling left now, then pivoting in a tight turn so that now it faced the front of the building. Without hesitation, it proceeded. Dub watched in horrified fascination as the high wall bowed, letting in wedges of dusty light, then burst outward. Dub and Mick ran from

the building and up the dusty street toward
the crowd in front of Kibbe's Feed Depot.

The New Orchard Defense Force (First Fencibles) was drawn up in two ragged ranks,
forty-three in number, including fourteen-year-
old Ted Plunkett, seventy-eight-year-old Jo-
seph Peters, and Mildred Fench, thirty-seven,
standing in for her husband Tod, indisposed
with a touch of an old malaria.

Chester (Pud) Boone, Colonel, CTVR, awkward in his tight-fitting uniform and reeking
of bromoform, took up a position some twenty
feet in front of the first rank, facing Private
Tim Peltier, a plump young fellow in dung-
stained coveralls.

" 'Smatter, Timmy, forget your pitchfork?"
Pud essayed comfortably. "Let's jest move off
smart, now," he went on in the sober tones of
command. "Round back, for issue of weapons."

"As you were," a strange voice cut authori-
tatively across the hubbub as the Fencibles
executed an approximate about-face and began to straggle off along the rutted street. The
troops halted, those behind colliding with those
before, and all heads turned to seek the source
of the order. Colonel Boone, bridling, strode
over to intercept the clean-shaven old man
who had countermanded his instructions. He
stared long at the seamed face and into the
pale blue eyes, only slightly bloodshot; surveyed the clean but ill-fitting pajama-like gar-
ment the newcomer wore; his examination

ended with the bare feet prominent below the frayed pants-cuff.

"Henry?" he inquired in a tone of total incredulity. "What call you got to go interfering with serious business? Now, you just go 'bout your business, Henry; we got a job o' work ahead of us here, got no time for fooling."

"Don't be a damned fool, Colonel," Henry responded firmly. "All you'll do is get these fellows killed. Those are Deng regulars out there, and there's armor coming up. You heard young McClusky's report. Now, dismiss this gang and let's get busy."

"By what right—" Boone started, but was cut off by the old fellow's surprising sharp reply.

"Used to be in the service; Marines, to be exact," Henry told the cowed reservist.

In the street, all heads turned as one toward the sudden *screech!* of tearing metal from the direction of the museum, and all eyes stared in disbelief as the snouts of the twin infinite repeaters thrust out through collapsing blue panels into daylight. They gazed, transfixed, as the vast machine emerged, shouldering the scattered façade aside to advance with the ponderous dignity of an irresistible force to the street, where it paused as if to orient itself while the remains of the museum collapsed gently behind it. Davis exited through the dust at a dead run, his corner office being the only portion of the structure not to fall.

*   *   *

"Here, what in damnation's going on?" Colonel Boone yelled.

"Stand fast," old Henry's voice cut across the cacophony of astonishment. "Looks like she's come out of retirement. I don't know how, but the timing is good!"

"Old Jonah'll take care of them spodders!" a middle-aged corporal shouted. "Three loud ones for old Jonah! Yippee!"

"At ease," Henry barked. "Look out there, Colonel," he advised Boone. "Better get your troops out of the street."

"Sure, Henry, I was jest . . ." the reservist faltered.

"Fall out!" Henry shouted over the din. "Form up in front of Lightner's!"

The bewildered Fencibles, grateful for authoritive guidance, broke up into a dozen small groups and headed across the street, all talking at once, their voices drowned out by rumbling as the mighty Bolo's treads pulverized the hard-rutted street surface, moving past them with the irresistibility of a moon in its orbit.

"—going right after 'em!"

"—here, where's it—my store!"

"Damn thing's going the wrong way! Damn spodders is *thataway!*"

A man ran a few steps after the combat unit as it angled abruptly right and crossed the walkway to doze aside the building which stood in its path, one of the older warehouses, trampling the old boards flat while its owner danced and yelled in frustrated fury.

"Hey, you damfool! Not that way, over here!" Cy Kibbe shouted, his voice lost in the splintering of seasoned timber.

As the townsfolk watched in astonishment, the old machine laid its track of destruction through the warehouse, taking off the near corner of the adjacent structure, and continued out across the formerly tilled acreage, trailing a tangle of metal piping and conduit ripped from the flattened buildings.

"It's running away!" someone blurted, voicing the common thought.

"Well, boys, it looks like we're on our own after all," Boone yelled, his voice overloud in the comparative hush. "Let's form up in a column of ducks here and go roust them damn spodders!"

"Stand fast!" Henry's command rang out, bringing movement to a halt. He strode across to take up a position between Boone and his disordered command.

"The enemy has zond projectors, and they've set up a z-beamer. Do you have any idea what those energy weapons can do to you? Now, fall out and go about your business."

"Not while I'm colonel," Boone shouted. "I don't know who you think you are, tryna give the orders around here, but we ain't going to jest stand by while a bunch of spodders take our land!"

"Just a minute," Davis' cool voice cut in, as

the government man stepped forward to confront Henry.

"You say you were a Marine, Mr. Henry. May I ask what your duties were in the Corps?"

"Sure," the old fellow replied promptly. "My duties was killing the enemy."

"I recall a case some twenty years ago," Davis said as if musing aloud. "It involved a much-decorated combat veteran who refused a direct order from the Council, and was cashiered." Davis glanced at Henry's face, set in an inscrutable expression.

"Wanted me to supervise burning out all our old combat veterns—combat units, I'm talking about," Henry said in an indignant tone. "Didn't need 'em anymore, the damned civilians figgered, so *I* was supposed to see they all had their cores melted down. Damned if I'd do it!" Henry spat past Davis' foot.

"His name, as I recall," Davis said imperturbably, "was Major General Thadeo Henry." He put out his hand. "I think all of us are glad now you got here in time to prevent the destruction of our old Jonah, General Henry."

Henry took the proffered hand briefly. "I was lucky on that one," he muttered. "I was just a 'misbegotten dog of a broken officer,' as Councilman Gracye put it, but the locals here were on my side. They run that demolition crew back where they came from. Good thing Spivey's is so far back in the boondocks; they never bothered with us after that. And now," he went on after a pause, "you're thinking a

Bolo fighting machine has run off and deserted in the face of the enemy. Not bloody likely."

At that moment, a staccato series of detonations punctuated the hush that had followed Henry's astonishing statement. Through the gap where the Bolo had passed the machine was visible half a mile distant now, surrounded by smaller enemy Yavac units, three of which were on fire. The others were projecting dazzling energy beams which converged on the Bolo, stationary now like a hamstrung bison surrounded by wolves. As the townfolk watched, the Bolo's forward turret traversed and abruptly spouted blue fire. A fourth Yavac exploded in flames.

"General Henry," Davis addressed the old man formally, "will you assume command for the duration of the emergency!"

Henry looked keenly at Boone and said, "Colonel, I trust you'll stay on and act as my adjutant." The reservist nodded awkwardly and stepped back.

"Sure I will," Henry told Davis firmly. "Now after old Jonah finishes with that bunch, he'll swing around and hit the advance party from the flank. Meantime, we lie low and don't confuse the issue."

"Right, General," Boone managed to gibber before turning with a yell to the disorganized crowd into which his command had dissolved.

"Ah, General," Davis put in diffidently. "Isn't there something constructive we could do to assist, rather than standing idly by, with all our hopes resting on an obsolete museum-piece?"

"The Deng have one serious failing, militarily, Mr. Davis," General Henry replied gravely. "Inflexibility—the inability to adjust promptly to changing circumstances. They're excellent planners—and having once decided on a tactical approach they ride it down in flames, so to speak. You've noticed that the forces concentrating on the west, behind the screen of the thicket, have made no move to support the main strike force now under attack to the east. They've taken up a formation suited only to an assault on the village here; when Jonah takes them in the flank, they'll break and run, simply because they hadn't expected it. Just watch."

Through the gap the Bolo had flattened in passing, the great machine was still visible within the dust-and-smoke cloud raised by the action. Five enemy hulks now sat inert and smouldering, while seven more were maneuvering on random evasive tracks that steadily converged on the lone Bolo, pouring in their fire without pause.

I select another enemy unit as my next target. These class C Yavac scouts are no mean opponents; clearly considerable improvement has been made in their circuitry during the two centuries of my absence from the field. Their armor withstands all but a .9998-accurate direct hit on the turret juncture. My chosen target—the squad leader, I compute—is a bold fellow who darts in as if to torment me. I track, lock onto him, and fire a long burst from my repeaters, even as I detect the first indications of excessive energy drain. My only option is to attune my charging grid to the frequency of the Yavac main batteries and invite their fire, thus permitting the enemy to recharge my plates—at the risk of overload and burn-out. It is a risk I must take. I fire what I compute is my last full-gain bolt at the enemy unit, at the same time receiving a revivifying jolt of energies in the Y-band as I take direct hits from two Yavacs. I am grateful for the accuracy of their fire, as well as for the sagacity of my designers, who thus equipped me to turn the enemy's strength against him—so long as my defensive armor and circuitry can withstand the overload. I see the squad leader erupt in fire, and change targets to the most aggressive of his subordinates. He was a bold opponent. I shall so report to my commander, taking due note of the fallen enemy's ID markings.

"Looky there! He done blowed up another one!" Hick Marlowe cried, pointing to the exploding Yavac which was already the focus of all eyes. "Look at old Jonah go! Bet he'll pick 'em off one at a time now till he gets the last one. But . . ." Hick paused, squinting through the obscuring dust, "he sure is taking a pasting his ownself—but he can handle it, old

Jonah can! He's starting to glow—must be hotter than Hell's hinges in there!"

"Can it stand up to that concentrated fire, General?" Davis asked the newly-appointed commander.

Henry nodded. "Up to a point," he muttered. "Depends on how much retrofit he got before they sent him out here. Now, this is top GUTS-information, Davis, but under the circumstances, I think you qualify as a 'Need to Know.' The new—or was new back in Ought-Four—defensive technology is to turn the enemy strength against him, by letting the Bolo absorb those hellish Y-rays, restructure them, and convert the energy into usable form to rebuild his own power reserve. But to do it he has to invite the enemy fire at close range—that's why he's sitting still—and take all the punishment that entails—if he can handle it without burnout. At best his 'pain' circuitry is under severe overload. Don't fool yourself, Davis. That's no fun, what Unit JNA is going through out there. Good boy! He took out another one, and now watch that fellow on the left, he's been getting pretty sassy, nipping in and out. My guess is he's next."

Standing on the porch of his ramshackle store with Freddy Frink, Mayor Kibbe wiped his broad brow and frowned. Even if the town survived this damn battle, things'd never be the same again. The last trickle of off-planet trade would die out if Spivey's became known

as a battleground, where the Deng could hit
anytime. Abruptly, he became aware of what
Frink was saying:

"—be worth plenty—the right stuff at the
right place, at the right time, Mr. Mayor. And
you're the only one's got it. Shame to let it go
to waste."

"What you talking about, Freddy?" Kibbe
demanded impatiently. "Town's getting blowed
apart practically, and you're worrying me about
wasting something. Stray shot hits the town,
whole thang's wasted—and you and me with
it."

"Sure, Mr. Mayor, that's what I'm talking
about," Frink came back eagerly. "Don't forget even if old Jonah runs these here spodders
off, they's still the main party back in the
Canyon. And Pud's idea was right: we can
blast the Rim right down on 'em."

"How we going to do that?" Kibbe challenged. "We been all over that. Ain't no way
to tote two hundredweight o' smashite up yonder onto the Rim."

"Old Jonah could do it, Cy," Frank urged.
"Could swing out into the badlands and come
up on the Cut from the northeast and get
right in position. Got the old mining road
comes down the face, you know."

"Bout halfway," Kibbe grunted. "He might
get down far enough to set the charge, but
how'd he get back up? No place to turn
around."

"I betcha a thousand guck a kilo wouldn't

be too much to expect," Frink suggested. "A hundred thousand, cash money—if we act quick."

"That's damn foolishness, Freddy," Kibbe countered. "You really think—a hundred thousand?"

"Minimum," Frink said firmly. "I guess you'd give a fellow ten percent got it all set up, eh, Mr. Mayor?"

"Old Jonah might not last out the day," Kibbe said more briskly. "Don't know where he got the recharge; he was drained dry before they built the museum around him, back in eighty-four. Can't last long out there." He half turned away.

"Wait a minute, Mr. Mayor," Frink said quickly. "Don't know what happened, but he's still going strong. He'll be back here pretty soon. All we got to do, we got to load that smashite in his cargo bay, wire it up fer remote control, and send him off. Works, we'll be heroes; don't work, makes no difference, we're finished here anyway. This way we got a kinder chance. But we got to move fast; don't want old Cabot to try to grab the credit. That's solid gold you got back in the shelves, Cy—*if* you use it right."

"Can't hurt none to try, I guess," Kibbe acknowledged, as if reluctantly. "Got to clear it with Davis and *General* Henry, too, I guess."

"Hah, some general," Frank sneered.

*   *   *

When Unit JNA had pounded the last of the dozen attacking Yavacs into silence, it moved past the burned-out hulks and directed its course to the west, bypassing the end of Main Street by a quarter mile, then just as the raptly observing townsfolk perched on roofs or peering from high windows had begun to address rhetorical questions to each other, it swung south and accelerated. At once fire arced from the north of the trees, where enemy implacements were concealed. The Bolo slowed and then halted to direct infilade fire into the crevasse, then resumed its advance, firing both main batteries rapidly now. A great gout of soil and shattered treetrunks erupted from mid-thicket. The bodies of Deng troopers were among the debris falling back to the ground.

"Smart, like I said," General Henry told Cy Kibbe, who had made his way up beside him. "He poured the fire into the zond-projector they had set up yonder, because he knew if he could boost it past critical level it'd blow, and take the heart out of 'em."

"Commendable, I'm sure, General," Kibbe commented. "But I'm afeared these niceties of military tactics are beyond me. Now, General—" Kibbe followed closely as Henry turned in at an alley to approach the scene of action more closely. "—me and some of the fellows are still quite concerned, General, about what we understand: that most of these dang Deng—" he broke off to catch his breath. "No

levity intended, sir," he interjected hastily—
"these infernal aliens, I meant to say—which
remain at Big Cut, with offensive power quite
intact!"

"As you said, Kibbe," Henry dismissed the
plump civilian, "these are matters you know
nothing about. I assure you I'm mindful that
the enemy has not yet committed his main
body. You may leave that to me." He walked
into the field, watching as the Bolo closed on
the now-gutted thicket, whence individual
Deng troopers were departing on foot, while
the few light Yavacs which had come up ma-
neuvered in the partial screen of the burning
woods to reform a blunt wedge, considerably
hindered by the continuing fire from their
lone antagonist. Then they, too, turned and
fled, getting off a few scattered Parthian shots
from their rear emplacements as they went.
Unit JNA trampled unhindered through the
splintered remains of the patch of trees, skirt-
ing the shallow gully at its center, and turned
toward town. A ragged cheer went up as the
huge machine rounded into Main Street and
crossed the last few yards to halt before the
clustered townsfolk. Davis thrust Dub forward.

People shrank back from the terrific heat
radiating from the battle-scarred machine, if
not from the terrifying aspect of its immense
bulk, the fighting prowess of which had just
been so vividly demonstrated before their eyes.

"Well done, Johnny," the boy said unsteadily.
"You can rest now."

"Jest a dadburned minute here," Kibbe burst out, pushing his way to the fore. "I guess ain't no mission accomplished while the main bunch o' them spodders is still out to Big Cut, safe and sound, and planning their next move!"

Henry came up beside Dub and put his hand on the boy's shoulder. "Your protégé did well, Dub," he said. "But the mayor has a valid point."

"Johnny done enough," Dub said doggedly.

"More than could have been expected," Henry agreed.

"Jest a dang minute, here," Cy Kibbe yelled. "I guess maybe us local people got something to say about it!" He turned to face the by-standers crowding in. "How about it—Bub, Charlie, you, Ben—you going to stand here while a boy and a—a ..." the momentum of his indignation expended, Kibbe's voice trailed off.

"A boy and 'a drunken derelict,' is I believe, the term you were searching for," Henry supplied. He, too faced the curious crowd. "Any suggestions?" he inquired in a discouraging tone.

"Durn right," a thin voice piped up promptly. Whiskery Fred Frink stepped to the fore, his expression as determined as his weak chin allowed. "Mr. Cabot, here, come up with a good idear," he went on. "Said let's load up this here museum-piece with some o' Mayor's explosives, left over from the last mining boom, you know, petered out all of a sudden, and send him out and blow that cliff right down on top of them spodders." Frink folded his arms and looked over his narrow shoulder for approval. General Henry frowned thoughtfully.

"Johnny's done enough," Dub repeated, tugging at the former town drunk's sleeve. "Let the mayor and some o' them go blow up the spodders."

"I'm afraid that's not practical, Dub," the general said gently. "I agree with the mayor that there are not enough fit men in town to carry out the mission, which I'm inclined to agree is our only option, under the circumstances. It's Unit JNA's duty to go where he's needed."

"You, boy," Frink yapped. "Tell this overgrowed tractor to pull up over front of the Depot."

Dub went casually over to confront the whiskery little man. Carefully, he placed his thumbs in his ears and waggled his fingers. Then he extended his tongue to its full length, looking Frink in the eye until the little man stepped back and began to bluster.

"Me, too, Dub," General Henry said, and pushed the boy gently toward the machine. Dub went as close to the Bolo as the still-hot metal would allow. "Listen, Johnny," he said earnestly. "They want you to go up on top the Badlands and plant some kind o' bomb. Can you do it?"

There was a moment of rapt silence from the open-mouthed crowd before the reply came clearly:

"As you wish, my commander. I compute that my energy reserve is sufficient to the task, though I am not fully combat-ready."

"Ain't gonna be no combat," Frink piped up. "Jest get the stuff in position, is all."

"Better go over by Kibbe's," Dub addressed the machine reluctantly. At once the vast bulk backed, scattering townsfolk, pivoted, and advanced to the indicated position, dwarfing the big shed.

"Tell it to open up," Frink commanded. Dub nodded and passed the order along to the Bolo; immediately the aft cargo hatch opened to reveal the capacious storage space beneath.

At Frink's urging, with Kibbe fussily directing the volunteers to the rear storage loft, a human chain formed up, and in moments the first of the bright-yellow, one-pound packages of explosive was passed along the line, and tucked away in the far corner of the Bolo's cargo bin.

As the last of the explosive was handed down to Frink, who had stationed himself inside the bin, stacking the smashite, Kibbe climbed up to peer inside cautiously before handing down a coil of waxy yellow wire, and a small black box marked DETONATOR, MARK XX.

"Got to rig it up fer remote control," he explained gratuitously to Henry, who was watching closely. "So's he can unload and back off before it goes up."

Half an hour later, while the entire population of New Orchard cheered, the battle-scarred machine once more set off across the plain toward the distant fault-line known as the Cliff. Dub stood with Henry, hoping that no one would notice the tears he felt trickling down his face.

"He'll be all right, son," Henry reassured the lad. "The route you passed on to him will take him well to the east, so that he'll come up on Big Cut directly above the enemy concentration."

"It ain't fair," Dub managed, furious at the break in his voice.

"It seems to be the only way," Henry told him. "There are lives at stake, Dub. Perhaps this will save them."

"Johnny's worth more'n the whole town," Dub came back defiantly.

"I can't dispute that," Henry said quietly. "But if all goes well, we'll save both, and soon Unit JNA will be back in his museum, once we rebuild it, with new battle honors to his credit. Believe me, this is as he wants it. Even if he should be ambushed, he'd rather go down fighting."

"He trusted me to look out for him," Dub insisted.

"There's nothing you could have done that would have pleased him more than ordering him into action," Henry said with finality. In silence, they watched the great silhouette dwindle until it was lost against the cliffs, misty with distance.

Once more I know the exultation of going on the offensive against a worthy foe. My orders, however, do not permit me to close with him, but rather to mount the heights and to blast the rock down on him. This, I compute, is indeed my final mission. I shall take care to execute it in a manner worthy of the Dinochrome Brigade. While the wisdom of this tactical approach is clear, it is not so satisfying as would be a direct surprise attack. Once at the Rim, I am to descend the cliff-face so far as is possible, via the roadway blasted long ago for access to certain mineral deposits exposed in the rockface. I am weary after this morning's engagement, nearing the advanced depletion level, but I compute that I have enough energy in reserve to carry out my mission. Beyond that, it is not my duty to compute.

Sitting at his desk, Cy Kibbe jumped in startlement when General Henry spoke suddenly, behind him. "I declare, Henry—I mean General," Kibbe babbled. "I never knowed—never seen you come in to my office here. What can I do for you, General, sir?'

"You can tell me more about this errand you've sent Unit JNA off on. For example, how did you go about selecting the precise point at which the machine is to set the charges?"

Kibbe opened a drawer and took out a sheaf of papers from which he extracted a hand-drawn map labeled *Claim District 33*, showing details of the unfinished road on the cliff face. After Henry had glanced at it, Kibbe produced glossy 8 × 10 photos showing broken rock, marked-up in red crayon.

"Got no proper printouts, sir," he explained hastily. "Jest these old pitchers and the sketch-map, made by my pa years ago. Shows the road under construction," Kibbe pointed to the top photo. "See, General, far as it goes, it's plenty wide enough for the machine."

"I don't see how it's going to turn around on that goat path," Henry commented, shuffling through the photos. "You loaded two hundred pounds of Compound L-547. That's enough to blow half the cliff off, but it has to be placed just right."

"Right, sir," Kibbe agreed eagerly. "Right at the end o' the track'll do it. I know my explosives, sir, used to be a soft-rocker myself, up till the vein played out. My daddy taught me. Lucky I had the smashite on hand; put good money into stocking it, and been holding it all these years."

"I'm sure the claim you put in to Budev will cover all that," Henry said shortly.

"Sir," Kibbe said in a more subdued tone, as he extracted another paper from the drawer. "If you'd be so kind, General, to sign this here emergency requisition form, so's to show I supplied the material needed for gubment business. . . ."

Henry looked at the document. "I suppose I can sign this," he acknowledged. "I saw the explosives loaded, looks legitimate to me." He took the stylus proffered by Kibbe and slashed an illegible signature in the space indicated.

"I understand you have an old observation station on the roof, for watching the mining work at the cliff," Henry said. "Let's go up and see how well we can monitor the Bolo's progress."

Kibbe agreed with alacrity, and led the way to the narrow stair which debouched on the tarred roof. He went across to a small hut, unlocked the door, and ushered the general into the stuffy interior crammed with old-fashioned electronic gear. He seated himself at the console and punched keys. A small screen lit up and flickered until Kibbe turned dials to steady an image of looming pinkish rock pitted with shallow cavities. "Blasted them test holes," he grunted. "Hadda abandon the work cause the formation was unstable, big mining engineer told Pa, condemned the claim—but that's just what we need, now!" Kibbe leaned back, grinning in satisfaction. "One good jolt, and the whole overburden'll come down. Now let's see can we get a line on the spodders down below the Cut." He twiddled knobs and the screen scanned down the rockface to the dry riverbed at the bottom, where the Deng had deployed their armor in battle array.

"Lordy," Kibbe whispered. "Got enough of 'em, ain't they Generalsir?"

"Looks like a division, at least," Henry agreed. "They're perfectly placed for your purposes, Mr. Mayor, if nothing alerts them."

"I suppose their transports are farther north in the cut," Henry said.

"That's right, Generalsir," Kibbe confirmed. "I been keeping an eye on 'em up here ever since we heard where they was at. Mighty handy, having this here spy gear." Kibbe patted the panel before him. "Pa suspicioned there was some dirty work going on at the claim, claim-jumpers and the like; spent a pretty penny shipping all this gear in and paid some experts to install it, placed the pick-up eyes all over to give him good coverage. Yessir, a pretty penny."

"I'll confirm the use of your equipment when you file your claim, Mr. Mayor," Henry said. "You'll make a nice profit on it. Provided," he added, "your plan works."

"Gotta work," Kibbe said, grinning. He adjusted the set again, and now it showed the approach to the cliff road, with the Bolo coming up fast, trailing a dustcloud that was visible now also through the lone window of the look-out shed.

The two men watched as the machine slowed, scouted the cliff-edge, then pivoted sharply, its prow dipping as it entered the man-made cut. Kibbe dollied in, and they watched the big machine move steadily down the rough-surfaced road, which was barely wide enough for passage by the Bolo.

"Close, but it's got room," Kibbe said. "Pa wasn't no dummy when he had 'em cut that trail wide enough for the heavy haulers."

"Very provident man, your father," Henry acknowledged. "I assume you'll include road-toll fees in your claim."

"Got a right to," Kibbe asserted promptly.

"Indeed you have," Henry confirmed. "I won't dispute your claim. A military man knows his rights, Mr. Mayor—but he also knows his duty."

"Sure," Kibbe said. "Well, I guess I done my duty all right, putting all my equipment and supplies at the disposal of the gubment and all—not to say nothing about the time I put in on this. I'm a busy man, General, got the store to run and the town, too, but I've taken the time off, like now, to see to it the public's needs is took care of."

"Your public spirit amazes me," Henry said in a tone which Kibbe was unable to interpret.

At that moment, the office door creaked and Kibbe turned to greet Fred Frink, who hesitated, his eyes on Henry.

"Come right on in, Freddy," Kibbe said heartily. "You're just in time. Looky here." He leaned back to afford the newcomer an unimpeded view of the screen where the Bolo had halted at a barrier of striated rock.

"End o' the road," Kibbe commented. "Perfect spot to blast that cliff right down on the durn spodders."

Frink was holding a small plastic keybox in his hand. He looked from Henry to Kibbe, a worried expression on his unshaven face.

"Go ahead, Freddy," Kibbe urged, as he snapped switches on the panel. "All set," he added. "You're on the air. Go." As he turned to catch Frink's eye, the scene on the screen exploded into a fireball shrouded in whirling dust. The great slab of rock blocking the road seemed to jump, then fissured and fell apart, separating into a multitude of ground-car-sized chunks which seemed to move languidly downward before disintegrating into a chaotic scene of falling rock and spurting dust, in which the Bolo was lost to view. As the dust thinned, settling, nothing was visible but a vast pit in the shattered rock-face, heaped rocks, and a rapidly dissipating smoke-cloud.

"We done it!" Kibbe exulted, while Frink stared at the screen, wide-eyed.

"I see now why you weren't concerned about how the unit would turn around to withdraw," Henry said in an almost lazy tone. "It's buried under, I'd estimate, a few thousand tons of pulverized limestone. Not that it matters much, considering what the explosion did to its internal circuitry. Not even a Bolo can stand up unharmed to a blast of that magnitude actually within its war-hull."

"Cain't make a omelette without you break

a few aigs," Kibbe said complacently, then busied himself at the panel. Again he scanned down the cliff-face, ending this time at a panorama of smoking rubble which filled the bottom of the Cut from wall to wall. Not a Yavac was to be seen.

"Don't reckon them spodders is going no place now, General," he commented complacently. Both men turned as Freddy uttered a yelp and turned and ran from the room, yelling the glad news. In moments, a mob-roar rose from the street below.

"Don't start celebrating just yet," General Henry said quietly, his eyes on the screen. Kibbe glanced at him, swallowed the objection he had been about to utter, and followed the general's glance. On the screen, almost clear of obscuring dust, the blanket of broken rock at the bottom of the Cut could be seen to heave and bulge. Great rocks rolled aside as the iodine-colored snout of a Class One Yavac emerged; the machine's tracks gained purchase; the enemy fighting machine dozed its way out from its premature burial and manuvered on the broken surface of the drift of rock to take up its assigned position, by which time two more heavy units had joined it, while the rubble was heaving in another half-dozen spots where trapped units strove to burst free. Forming up in the deep wedge specified, Henry knew, by Deng battle regs, the salvaged machines moved off toward the south and the defenseless town.

"It appears we'll have to evacuate after all," Henry said quietly. "I shall ask Mr. Davis to get off an emergency message to Sector. I can assign a GUTS priority to it, and I think we should have help within perhaps thirty-six hours. I'm no longer on the Navy list, but I still know the old codes."

"That'd be Wednesday," Kibbe said, rising hastily. "Best they can do, General?"

"Considering the distance to the nearest installation capable of mounting a relief mission, thirty-six hours is mildly optimistic, Mr. Mayor. We'll just have to hold out somehow."

There was a sound of hurrying feet, and the door slammed wide as Dub arrived, flushed and panting.

"We seen the big dust-cloud, General Henry," he gasped out. "Is Johnny OK?"

Henry went to the boy and put a fatherly hand on his shoulder. "Johnny did his duty as a soldier, Dub," he said gently. "It's to be expected that there will be casualties."

"What's a casualty mean?" Dub demanded, looking up at the old man.

"It means old Jonah done his job and got himself kilt, as you might say, boy." Cy Kibbe said lazily. Dub went past him to stare at the screen.

"He's under that?" he asked fearfully.

"The grave will be properly marked, Dub," Henry reassured the lad. "His sacrifice will not go unnoticed."

"*They* done it," Dub charged pointing at

Kibbe and Frink, now cowering behind the mayor. "I ast Mr. Frink, how Johnny was going to unload the smashite and put it in the right place, and he didn't even answer me." The boy began to cry, hiding his face.

"No call to take on, boy," Frink spoke up. "All I done was what I hadda do. Nobody'd blame me." He looked almost defiantly at Henry.

"You could of gone along and unloaded the stuff, instead of blowing Johnny up," Dub charged. "You didn't hafta go and kill him." He advanced on Frink, his fists clenched.

"Now boy, after all it's only a dang machine we're talking about," Kibbe put in, moving to block Dub's approach to Frink. "A machine doing what it was built to do. You can't expect a man to go out there and get himself kilt, too."

Dub turned away and went to the screen, on which could now be seen the slope of rubble, from the floor of the canyon to the aborted road far above, with the great black cavity of the blast site.

"Look!" Dub exclaimed, pointing. Beside the blast pit, rocks were shifting, thrust aside; small stones dribbled down the talus slope— and then the prow of the Bolo appeared, dozing its way out from under the heaped rock fragments, a gaping wound visible where its aft decking was ripped open.

"He's still alive!" Dub cried. "Come on, Johnny! You can do it!"

*   *   *

I am disoriented by the unexpected blast. Assessing the damage, I perceive that it was not a hit from enemy fire, but rather that the detonation originated in my cargo bin. Belatedly, I realize that I was loaded with explosives and dispatched on a suicide mission. I am deeply disturbed. The Code of the Warrior would require that my commander inform me fully of his intention. This smacks of treachery. Still, it is not for me to judge. Doubtless he did what was necessary. Yet I am grieved that my commander did not feel that he could confide in me. Did he imagine I would shirk my duty? I have suffered grievous damage, but my drive train at least is intact. I shall set aside .003 nanoseconds to carry out a complete self-assessment . . .

Happily, my hatch cover blew first, as designed, thus venting the greater part of the pressure harmlessly into the surrounding rock. My motor circuits are largely intact, though I have suffered serious loss of sensitivity in my sensory equipment. Still, if I can extricate myself from the entrapping rubble, I compute that I have yet sufficient energy—my Y grid having absorbed some two hundred mega-ergs from the blast and converted the simple kinetic force into usable C-energies—to extricate myself and report to base. I sense the overburden shifting as I apply pressure; now I emerge into sunlight. The way is clear before me. I descend the slope, taking care not to initiate an avalanch. It is clear that I will never again know my full potency, but I shall do what I can.

* * *

General Henry shouldered Freddy Frink aside and commandeered the chair before the remote view-screen in Kibbe's observation shed, now crowded with excited villagers, all talking at once, all anxious as to their impending fate.

"... do it? Are they going to be able to climb out?"

"... things come over that heap! Can you see them?"

Manning the small telescope mounted at a window and commanding a view of the terrain where the Yavacs would appear if they indeed succeeded in climbing clear of the fallen cliff's debris, Bud Tolliver maintained a running commentary.

"—see one of 'em—big fellow, lots bigger'n those little ones old Jonah tangled with. There's another one. They keep on coming. Blasting the cliff didn't do no good, it looks like. They're headed thisaway. Our museum-piece is way behind."

In a brief lull, Henry spoke up:

"Only the heavies apparently are able to dig out. Three, so far—and they appear to be sluggish. No doubt they suffered concussive damage at a minimum."

"Can I look?" Young Dub crowded in and Henry took the boy onto his lap.

"Where's Johnny?" the boy demanded, staring at the screen. "Hard to make out what's

happening, Mr.—General Henry. You said he
started downslope, but—"

"There he is," Henry cut in, pointing to
a dust trail near the edge of the screen. "He's
going to try to outflank them and beat them
into the open."

"Think he can do it, sir?" Dub begged.

"He'll do his best," Henry reassured the
boy. "It's his duty to return to base and report."

*I win clear of the blast area, and by channel-
ing all available energy to my drive train, I shall
attempt to gain egress from the Cut in advance
of the enemy units which I perceive have succeeded, like myself, in digging out. They, too, are
sluggish and as they slow to maneuver around a
major rock fragment; I steal a march and clear
the Cut and am in the open. It is only a short
dash now to base. Yet I am a fighting machine of
the Concordiat, with some firepower capability
remaining. Shall I withdraw in the face of the
enemy?*

"It's clear," General Henry said. "Incredible that a machine could withstand such a
blast—treacherously planted within his hull—
and still retain the ability to return to base—to
say nothing of digging out from under thirty
feet of rock."

"Did I hear you say something about treachery, Henry?" Kibbe demanded truculently. "I
guess maybe the gubment won't see it that
way. I guess it'll say I was a patriot, did what

he could to save the town and maybe the whole durn planet."

"Dang right," Fred Frink chimed in. "How about it, Mr. Davis?" He sought out the eye of the government man in the crowd. "Are me and Cy traitors, or what?"

"The matter will be investigated, you may be sure, Fred," Davis replied coolly. "The matter of planting a bomb within the unit without authorization is questionable at best."

"Ha!" Frink cried. "Jest because some kid and a broke-down ex-soldier got all wet-eyed about that piece o' junk—"

"That's enough from you," Henry said, and put his hand in the noisy fellow's face and shoved him backward. Frink sat down hard, looked up at Henry resentfully.

"I orter get one o' them medals, me and Cy, too," he grumped.

"I told you to shut your big mouth, Frink," Henry cut him off. "Next time it will be my boot in your face."

Frink subsided. Kibbe eased up beside Henry.

"Don't pay no mind to Freddy, Generalsir," he said, "he don't mean no harm." Kibbe glanced at Frink cowering on the floor.

"Guess now old Jonah'll skedaddle back here to town," Kibbe rambled on, watching the screen. "He got out ahead o' them spodder machines; he's in the clear."

"It would serve you right if he did," General Henry said coldly. "But look: After all he's been through, he's preparing to ambush them as they come out. Instead of using the last of his energy reserve to run for cover, he's attacking a superior force."

"Don't do it, Johnny," Dub begged. "You done all you could for them, and they paid you back by blowing you up. To heck with 'em. Run for it, and save yourself. I'll see you get repaired!"

"Even if he could hear you," Henry told the boy, "that's one order he'd ignore. His destiny is to fight and, if need be, to die in combat."

"Damn fool," Kibbe said. "It ain't got a chance against them three Yavac heavies."

On the screen, the Bolo was seen to enter a wide side crevasse and come to rest. A moment later, the first Yavac appeared and at once erupted in fire as the Bolo blasted it at close range with its main battery of Hellbores. The next two Deng machines veered off and took up divergent courses back to the Cut.

"They'll stand off and bombard," Henry said. "I think Unit JNA has exhausted his energies. But of course, if their fire is accurate, he can absorb a percentage of it and make use of it to recharge. They don't know that, or they'd simply bypass him. Instead, he's got them bottled up. Even in death, he's protecting us."

It was an hour after the first ship of the Terran Relief Force had arrived. After Henry had briefed the captain commanding, he returned to Dub, who, with Mick, had been awaiting his return at the hastily tidied office of the Planetary Rep.

"I think we can be sure," Davis told them, after an exchange of SWIFT messages with Sector, "that the museum will be rebuilt promptly, better than ever, and that Unit JNA will be fully restored and recommissioned as a Historic Monument in perpetuity. And his commander will, of course, have free access to him to confer any time he wishes."

"That's good," Dub said soberly. "I'll see to it he's never lonely again."

My young commander has been confirmed in the rank of Battle Captain, and, after depot maintenance and upgrading to modern specifications, I have been recommissioned as a Fighting Unit of the Line. This carries with it permanent full stand-by alert status, an energy level at which my memory storage files are fully available to me, as are also my extensive music and literary archives. Thus, I have been enabled to renew my study of the Gilgamesh epic, including all the new cuneiform material turned up in recent years at Nippur. The achievements of the great heroes of Man are an inspiration to me and should the Enemy again attack, I shall be ready.

A SHORT HISTORY
OF THE
BOLO
FIGHTING MACHINES

THE FIRST APPEARANCE in history of the concept of the armored vehicle was the use of wooden-shielded war wagons by the reformer John Huss in fifteenth-century Bohemia. Thereafter the idea lapsed—unless one wishes to consider the armored knights of the Middle Ages, mounted on armored war-horses—until the twentieth century. In 1915, during the Great War, the British developed in secrecy a steel-armored motor car; for security reasons during construction it was called a "tank," and the appellation remained in use for the rest of the century. First sent into action at the Somme in A.D. 1916 (BAE 29), the new device was immensely impressive and was soon copied by all belligerents. By Phase Two of the Great War, A.D. 1939–1945, tank corps were a basic element in all modern armies. Quite naturally, great improvements were soon made over the original clumsy, fragile, feeble, and temperamental tank. The British Sheridan and Centurion, the German Tiger, the American Sherman, and the Russian T-34 were all highly potent weapons in their own milieu.

During the long period of cold war following A.D. 1945, development continued, especially in the United States. By 1989 the direct ancestor of the Bolo line had been constructed by the Bolo Division of General Motors. This machine, at one hundred fifty tons almost twice the weight of its Phase Two predecessors, was designated the Bolo Mark I Model B. No Bolo Model A of any mark ever existed, since it was felt that the Ford Motor Company had preempted that designation permanently. The same is true of the name "Model T."

The Mark I was essentially a bigger and better conventional tank, carrying a crew of three and, via power-assisted servos, completely manually operated, with the exception of the capability to perform a number of preset routine functions such as patrol duty with no crew aboard. The Mark II that followed in 1995 was even more highly automated, carrying an on-board fire-control computer and requiring only a single operator. The Mark III of 2020 was considered by some to be almost a step backward, its highly complex controls normally requiring a crew of two, though in an emergency a single experienced man could fight the machine with limited effectiveness. These were by no means negligible weapons systems, their individual firepower exceeding that of a contemporary battalion of heavy infantry, while they were of course correspondingly heavily armored and shielded. The outer durachrome war hull of the Mark III was twenty millimeters thick and capable of withstanding any offensive weapon then known, short of a contact nuclear blast.

The first completely automated Bolo, designed to operate normally without a man aboard, was the landmark Mark XV Model M, originally dubbed *Resartus* for obscure reasons, but later officially named *Stupendous*. This model, first commissioned in the twenty-fifth century, was widely used throughout the Eastern Arm during the Era of Expansion and remained in service on remote worlds for over two centuries, acquiring many improvements in detail along the way while remaining basically unchanged, though increasing sophistication of circuitry and weapons vastly upgraded its effectiveness. The Bolo *Horrendous* Model R, of 2807 was the culmination of this phase of Bolo development, though older models lingered on in the active service of minor powers for centuries.

Thereafter the development of the Mark XVI–XIX consisted largely in further refinement and improvement in detail of the Mark XV. Provision continued to be made for a human occupant, now as a passenger rather than an operator, usally an officer who wished to observe the action at first hand. Of course, these machines normally went into action under the guidance of individually prepared computer programs, while military regulations continued to require installation of devices for halting or even self-destructing the machine at any time. This latter feature was mainly intended to prevent capture and hostile use of the great machine by an enemy. It was at this time that the first-line Bolos in Terran service were organized into a brigade, known as the Dinochrome Brigade, and deployed as a strategic unit. Tactically the regiment was the basic Bolo unit.

The always-present though perhaps unlikely possibility of capture and use of a Bolo by an enemy was a constant source of anxiety to military leaders and, in time, gave rise to the next and final major advance in Bolo technology: the self-directing (and, quite incidentally, self-aware) Mark XX Model B Bolo *Tremendous*. At this time it was customary to designate each individual unit by a three-letter group indicating hull style, power unit, and main armament. This gave rise to the custom of forming a nickname from the letters, such as "Johnny" from JNY, adding to the tendency to anthropomorphize the great fighting machines.

The Mark XX was at first greeted with little enthusiasm by the High Command, who now professed to believe that an unguided-by-operator Bolo would potentially be capable of running amok and wreaking destruction on its owners. Many observers have speculated by hindsight that a more candid objection would have been that the legitimate area of command function was about to be invaded by mere machinery. Machinery the Bolos were, but never *mere*.

At one time an effort was made to convert a number of surplus Bolos to peacetime use by such modifications as the addition of a soil-moving blade to a Mark XII Bolo WV/I Continental Siege Unit, the installation of seats for four men, and the description of the resulting irresistible force as a "tractor." This idea came to naught, however, since the machines retained their half-megaton/second firepower and were never widely accepted as normal agricultural equipment.

As the great conflict of the post-thirtieth-century era wore on—a period variously known as the Last War and, later, as the Lost War—Bolos of Mark XXVIII and later series were organized into independently operating brigades that did their own strategic as well as tactical planning. Many of these machines still exist in functional condition in out-of-the-way corners of the former Terran Empire. At this time the program of locating and neutralizing these ancient weapons continues.

KILLER STATION
by Martin Caidin

Several years from now we will be in the age of the great space station. The Congress of the U.S. has authorized funding and construction of a huge manned facility to orbit the Earth. We have already flown a great station in our old Skylab.

In a novel of deep human interaction and powerful forces, Martin Caidin has created that time when the huge *Pleiades* space station with 52 men and women is circling the Earth. But not even a berth 346 miles high can escape the power-hungry machinations of men and women in space, or on the Earth so far below them. Nor can this marvel of science, engineering, and politics escape the realities of a sun gone violent in its cycle of solar storms and flares that threatens the lives of all aboard, and, finally, the lives of millions of people on the planet below.

RUSH CANTRELL, station commander, and CHRISTY GORDON, a beautiful woman and leading scientist, pit their dominant personalities one against the other in this highest of human arenas. It is a deep-felt conflict between military and scientific needs, compounded by the attempt of a Soviet agent to destroy the great station through sabotage.

In a nonstop cliffhanger, the author sweeps the reader faster and faster toward the catastrophic outcome of this fierce struggle in space—with the survival of the nation's largest city poised in the balance.

Martin Caidin, who carved out an incredibly accurate portrayal of the future with his novel *Marooned*, and then his book and TV series *The Six Million Dollar Man* and *The Bionic Woman*, has created another slashing and emotion-wracked trip to another near future that promises all too soon to become reality.

Marooned . . . *Cyborg* . . . "The Six Million Dollar Man" . . . *The Last Command*—movies, television and books—Martin Caidin Writes The Big Ones. Now Caidin has outdone even Caidin: Here are some excerpts from one of the most exciting future thrillers of this or any year, **KILLER STATION**, a barely fictional novel of the near future brought with gut-wrenching impact to *now*!

Rush feared he would be too late. *Pleiades* shuddered with a renewed sickening motion. There could be no mistaking that dangerous wobble, no escaping the deep groaning sounds emitted by the enormous strains on the structure. A shrill alarm stabbed his ears and the emergency speakers sounded through the station.

"Red alert! Red alert! All hands! All hands! Pressure seal break in the station! Pressure seal break! All emergency crews on the double in suits to Tube Three, repeat, all emergency crews on the double in suits to Tube Three."

There came a momentary pause as if the speaker was trying to get his wits together—no, it was a woman's voice, Rush realized, Dianne Vecchio. "We are on full alert," she went on, calmer now. "All personnel into pressure suits immediately. All personnel into pressure suits immediately."

Rush saw Steve Longbow just outside Control. "Steve! Get your crews into their suits and then get some fireaxes and cut those goddamned cables from the computer! We can't wait for the lasers!"

He saw Longbow gesture to acknowledge the command and then Rush was jerked roughly by the shoulder. He flailed wildly with his arms to regain his balance, then saw Christy just behind him. "Get into your suit!" she screamed at him.

Beyond Christy's face lights flashed wildly and he saw plumes of the nontoxic red smoke released automatically whenever the pressure dropped. The smoke would follow any air leak and indicate just where they would find the breach in pressure seal. And the triple-damned smoke *was moving*, snaking its way through the air, showing long tendrils in a spiraling motion . . .

Maybe finality brought its own calm, he thought. The air was still screaming from the station, but far worse was that continuing thunder of the propulsion units, the rocking and agonized groaning of the station as unequal forces kept trying to tear it into great chunks. The crews cutting frantically with axes and steel bars must be making some progress. He could see showers of sparks and smoke boiling away where metal crashed into cables alive with electrical energy. Curses and shouts and then a shriek came from someone as they took a severe electrical jolt. The others kept working, and he confirmed they were chopping into power. The thrusters were cutting in and out, a barking cough of power, an intermittent burning of propulsion units even more devastating than full thrust because asymmetrical forces could twist them apart like wheat stalks in a farmer's hands.

The thunder stopped. They'd done it. "Okay, everybody. Grab patch kits. Let's seal this goddamned tin can."

The alarms that had clamored so loudly before were now barely audible in the thinning air; the next explosion boomed through the station like a rolling earth shock. Without atmosphere surrounding *Pleiades* the blast was confined to the pressurized interior, and even as they heard and felt the concussion through what was left of the air and structure of their space home they knew they'd been suckered not once but twice: Jill Brody had gutted the nuclear reactor and sabotaged their computer, but it had never occurred to them that they'd been double-teamed.

Rush Cantrell had frozen for only a moment, taking in all the sensations and then throwing himself forward to hit the manual backup alarms for all hands to don their emergency pressure suits. Again Christy Gordon was by his side, as was Sam Hammil, the three of them overseeing the emergency preparations to convert shuttle tanks as impromptu lifeboats should they have to abandon the station before the shuttles could rendezvous. In their suits they worked their way back to control central to assess the damage.

Everyone was already hair-triggered for any eventuality, and emergency patches had been slapped to new leaks. The core withstood the blast better than expected, and in moments they knew what had happened . . .

* * *

It was calamitous. Over a thousand tons of space station surviving the punch back into atmosphere and smashing into a populated area of more than fourteen million human beings couldn't be anything less than that. "Let's have the rest," Rush said finally.

They gave him the rest. They could expect the final swing into atmosphere over Asia, where they'd get the first .05-g reading. That meant resistance by atmosphere to their speed, a tremendously fast buildup of friction, and *Pleiades* would come arcing steeper and steeper toward the waiting earth below. Full reentry would be under way at approximately sixty degrees latitude north and the calculated drag profile ended up dead-center in the New York area.

It wasn't just New York as a city. It was the enormous, sprawling megapolis of New York, Long Island, Westchester County, and the solid line of cities of New Jersey. CapCom was still talking, he realized. They were talking about precautions being taken earthside. ". . . business end of Manhattan completely closed down until we complete reentry and impact . . . impossible to evacuate . . . logistics would be insane . . . lower Manhattan has a working-day population density of eight hundred fifty thousand people per square mile . . . got to remember that if we—" Another explosion rocked *Pleiades* . . .

* * *

The bastard's blown out the lab wall . . . explosive decompression. He's trying to blow us out of the station . . .

Rush loosened the cable at his waist as screaming air dragged him toward the gaping rupture in the module wall. Instead of fighting to keep his place, Rush threw himself forward. The outward-exploding pressure helped carry his body in the unexpected lunge, the laser saw extended before him. In seconds the vapor clouds cleared and he had an open shot at Sam's faceplate. Rush squeezed the laser-saw trigger and a blinding light stabbed forth.

No weapon, no cutting edge. Blinding light, and the eye-stabbing glare was his weapon. For the moment Sam Hammil couldn't see. Blinded by the searing light he threw up an arm instinctively to protect his eyes. He couldn't see Rush, who braced himself carefully and brought up his boot with all his strength to crash into Sam's groin. They heard his shriek of pain through the radio and saw his mouth open as he tried to suck in air. As he doubled over Rush brought the laser saw smashing as hard as he could into the lexan faceplate. It stunned Sam. Rush had just enough time to twist the laser saw dial to full cutting intensity of one-foot distance. He thrust the saw against the helmet and squeezed the trigger.

A thin beam of powerful light sliced through the lexan and into the flesh and bone just beyond. Another burst of vapor whipped through the compartment as the pressure seal of Sam's suit ruptured and the suit collapsed against his body. Blood burst from his nose and ears and mouth and the hole drilled into his cheekbone by the laser. He screamed silently, pink froth bubbling and spraying from his mouth, and with a desperate, dying lunge he grasped Rush's suit and dragged them both to the gaping hole in the module rim.

Both men tumbled helplessly into vacuum, out into certain death. Rush didn't bother to struggle. He felt Sam's body jerking wildly in his final seconds of life, then arch violently and go limp. They were turning as they floated from the station and then the cable connecting his suit with Christy pulled taut. His outward movement ended. Sam's body, trailing a faint pink cloud, drifted away.

"Just hold tight in there," Rush called to Christy. "I'll pull myself back in." He eased back into the module, careful of the jagged metal, and was then safely inside. A sobbing Christy threw herself into his arms. Rush took a long, shuddering breath.

Too close, too close!

*   *   *

... Rush didn't hesitate. "Okay, I'm coming in with the maneuvering engines." Far behind them, in the boattail section of *Falcon*, small rocket engines spat flame with perfect diamond-shaped shock waves back from the shuttle. The thunder and vibration increased.

"She won't take it, damn you!" Logan shouted.

"That's what we're going to find out," Rush told him coldly. "Okay, I'm coming up on the maneuvering engine throttles. Steady as she goes, nice and steady," talking now as much to himself as he was to anyone else, his hand on the throttles moving with infinite care. "Blake, you override me. I don't want any fast boost. Bring them in with me just as slow as they'll take the additional power."

Blake worried the throttles from his side of the flight deck and the new thunder was sharper, louder, more commanding. Metal groaned through *Falcon* as stresses built swiftly through the grappling arms. They were all asking the same questions of themselves. Will there be so much power that the grappling arms would fail? Would they simply snap? Would they twist and throw them wildly off balance? That could tear them loose from their fragile grip on *Pleiades* and bring *Falcon* smashing upward into the main structure of the station core. There was the rub. *Falcon* using her main engines had power to spare to nudge the enormous mass of *Pleiades* but they couldn't translate that power through the spindly structure of the grappling arms. Still the thunder continued.

"We're starting to show incremental velocity," Blake said, almost in a hush. "It's low *but it's there*. Goddamn, we're doing it, *we're doing it*, we're—"

"*BACK OFF! BACK OFF!*" Logan's voice was almost a scream. "The grapples have snapped!

Both of them! For God's sake, *BACK HER OFF!*''

Falcon shuddered, lurched slightly, and that alone could be a killer move. Rush killed the maneuvering engines with a single backward tug on the throttles, his fingers supersensitive tendrils on the controls. Pale flame spat from the nose and aft sections of *Falcon* as he reversed the attitude thrusters. They heard a grinding, crumpling roar and saw metal tumbling wildly, twisting like paper, directly ahead and above the flight deck windows. Rush looked up from the nose with a feeling of utter despair. *They had almost done it.* But it didn't work and the sand in the orbital hourglass was running out . . .

* * *

Pleiades came screaming down from the heavens with the wrath of an angry, even a maddened god, fourteen hundred tons crashing with terrifying impact into an atmosphere transformed by speed and resistance into protesting liquid metal. The lesser portions of the great space station, antenna and solar panels, loosened modules and observation blisters heated swiftly, glowed red and orange and then white, shredding away from the mass of the disintegrating station, incinerating themselves in an incredible, heart-grabbing display of silent screams, a thousand meteoroids, vividly colored through all the spectrum, flaring and twinkling and exploding without sound.

The greater bulk and size of *Pleiades* tore itself apart in this manner, spitting a thousand fireballs and brands, all rushing madly through the upper atmosphere like a comet loosely organized and burning to extinction. Larger fireballs preceded the wilder fiery conglomeration, burning in red and blue and orange and white and yellow and green, a mass of blazing debris such as the world had never seen. These were the heavier elements of *Pleiades'* final gasp of life, the astrophysics laboratory and the photo-mobile, and the astronomical observatory and pieces of airlock and, above all, that terrible mass of the nuclear reactor, the five hundred tons of burning, glowing, melting, exploding radioactive hell.

Pleiades shrieked across Canada and the Great Lakes and descended to lower heights over New Jersey with a shattering, rending sonic boom, a roar beyond all thunders, with clamorous shrieks of lesser flames. The dying station whipped across the metropolitan area on both sides of the Hudson River and across Long Island with the petrified, mesmerized millions of people watching the Sword of Damocles poised in those awful moments above their heads. The blazing chunks whipped to all sides and above and below the now completely fire-enveloped mass of the nuclear reactor, a star unto itself surrounded by hordes of lesser flames.

Available December 1985 from Baen Books
55996-6 • 384 pp. • $3.50

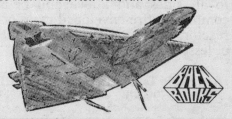

Here is an excerpt from Cobra
Strike!, *coming in February 1986
from Baen Books:*

The Council of Syndics—its official title—had in
the early days of colonization been just that: a some-
what low-key grouping of the planet's syndics and
governor-general which met at irregular intervals to
discuss any problems and map out the general direction in which they hoped the colony would grow. As
the population increased and beachheads were established on two other worlds, the Council grew in
both size and political weight, following the basic
pattern of the distant Dominion of Man. But unlike
the Dominion, this outpost of humanity numbered
nearly three thousand Cobras among its half-million
people.

The resulting inevitable diffusion of political power
had had a definite impact on the Council's makeup.
The rank of governor had been added between the
syndic and governor-general levels, blunting the pin-
nacle of power just a bit; and at *all* levels of government the Cobras with their double vote were well
represented.

Corwin Moreau didn't really question the political
philosophy which had produced this modification of
Dominion structure; but from a purely utilitarian
point of view he often found the sheer size of the
75-member Council unwieldy.

Today, though, at least for the first hour, things
went smoothly. Most of the discussion—including
the points Corwin raised—focused on older issues
which had already had the initial polemics thoroughly
wrung out of them. A handful were officially given
resolution, the rest returned to the members for more
analysis, consideration, or simple foot-dragging; and
as the agenda wound down it began to look as if the
meeting might actually let out early.

And then Governor-General Brom Stiggur dropped
a pocket planet-wrecker into the room.

It began with an old issue. "You'll all remember
the report of two years ago," he said, looking around
the room, "in which the Farsearch team concluded

that, aside from our three present worlds, no planets exist within at least a 20-light-year radius of Aventine that we could expand to in the future. It was agreed at the time that our current state of population and development hardly required an immediate resolution of this long-term problem."

Corwin sat a bit straighter in his seat, sensing similar reactions around him. Stiggur's words were neutral enough, but something explosive seemed to be hiding beneath the carefully controlled inflections of his voice.

"However," the other continued, "in the past few days something new has come to light, something which I felt should be presented immediately to this body, before even any follow-up studies were initiated." Glancing at the Cobra guard standing by the door, Stiggur nodded. The man nodded in turn and opened the panel ... and a single Troft walked in.

A faint murmur of surprise rippled its way around the room, and Corwin felt himself tense involuntarily as the alien made its way to Stiggur's side. The Trofts had been the Worlds' trading partner for nearly 14 years now, but Corwin still remembered vividly the undercurrent of fear that he'd grown up with. Most of the Council had even stronger memories than that: the Troft occupation of the Dominion worlds Silvern and Adirondack had occurred only 43 years ago, ultimately becoming the impetus for the original Cobra project. It was no accident that most of the people who now dealt physically with the Troft traders were in their early twenties. Only the younger Aventinians could face the aliens without wincing.

The Troft paused at the edge of the table, waiting as the Council members dug out translator-link earphones and inserted them. One or two of the younger syndics didn't bother, and Corwin felt a flicker of jealousy as he adjusted his own earphone to low volume. He'd taken the same number of courses in catertalk as they had, but it was obvious that foreign language comprehension wasn't even close to being his forté.

"Men and women of the Cobra Worlds Council," the earphone murmured to him. "I am Speaker One of the Tlos'khin'fahi demesne of the Trof'te Assemblage." The alien's high-pitched catertalk continued for a second beyond the translation; both races had early on decided that the first three parasyllables of Troft demesne titles were more than adequate for human use, and that a literal transcription of the aliens' proper names was a waste of effort. "The Tlos'khin'fahi demesne-lord has sent your own demesne-lord's request for data to the other parts of the Assemblage, and the result has been a triad offer from the Pua'lanek'zia and Baliu'ckha'spmi demesnes."

Corwin grimaced. He'd never liked deals involving two or more Troft demesnes, both because of the delicate political balance the Worlds often had to strike and because the humans never heard much about the Troft-Troft arm of such bargains. That arm *had* to exist—the individual demesnes seldom if ever gave anything away to each other.

The same line of thought appeared to have tracked its way elsewhere through the room. "You speak of a triad, instead of a quad offer," Governor Dylan Fairleigh spoke up. "What part does the Tlos'khin'fahi demesne expect to play?"

"My demesne-lord chooses the role of catalyst," was the prompt reply. "No fee will be forthcoming for our role." The Troft fingered something on his abdomen sash and Corwin's display lit up with a map showing the near half of the Troft Assemblage. Off on one edge three stars began blinking red. "The Cobra Worlds," the alien unnecessarily identified them. A quarter of the way around the bulge a single star, also outside Troft territory, flashed green. "The world named Qasama by its natives. They are described by the Baliu'ckha'spmi demesne-lord as an alien race of great potential danger to the Assemblage. Here—" a vague-edge sphere appeared at the near side of the flashing green star—"somewhere, is a tight cluster of five worlds capable of supporting human life. The Pua'lanek'zia demesne-lord will give you their location and an Assemblage pledge of human possession if your Cobras will undertake to eliminate the threat of Qasama. I will await your decision."

The Troft turned and left . . . and only slowly did Corwin realize he was holding his breath. Five brand-new worlds . . . for the price of becoming mercenaries.

Here is an excerpt from Fred Saberhagen's newest novel, coming in February 1986 from Baen Books:

FRED SABERHAGEN
THE
FRANKENSTEIN
PAPERS

Chapter 1

May? 1782?

I bite the bear.

I bit the bear.

I have bitten the white bear, and the taste of its blood has given me strength. Not physical strength—that I have never lacked—but the confidence to manage my own destiny, insofar as I am able.

With this confidence, my life begins anew. That I may think anew, and act anew, from this time on I will write in English, here on this English ship. For it seems, now that I try to use that language, that my command of it is more than adequate. Though how that ever came to be, God alone can know.

How *I* have come to be, God perhaps does not know. It may be that that knowledge is, or was, reserved to one other, who has—or had—more right than God to be called my Creator.

My first object in beginning this journal is to cling to the fierce sense of purpose that has been reborn in me. My second is to try to keep myself sane. Or to restore myself to sanity, if, as sometimes seems to me likely, madness is indeed the true explanation of the situation, or condition, in which I find myself—in which I believe myself to be.

But I verge on babbling. If I am to write at all—and I must write—let me do so coherently.

I have bitten the white bear, and the blood of the bear has given me life. True enough. But if anyone who reads is to understand then I must write of other matters first.

Yes, if I am to assume this task—or therapy—of journal-keeping, then let me at least be methodical about it. A good way to make a beginning, I must believe, would be to give an objective, calm description of myself, my condition, and my surroundings. All else, I believe—I must hope—can be built from that.

As for my surroundings, I am writing this aboard a ship, using what were undoubtedly once the captain's notebook and his pencils. The captain was wise not to trust that ink would remain unfrozen.

I am quite alone, and on such a voyage as I am sure was never contemplated by the captain, or the owners, or the builders of this stout vessel, *Mary Goode*. (The bows are crusted a foot thick with ice, an accumulation perhaps of decades; but the name is plain on many of the papers in this cabin.)

A fire burns in the captain's little stove, warms my fingers as I write, but I see by a small sullen glow of sunlight emanating from the south—a direction that here encompasses most of the horizon. Little enough of that sunlight finds its way in through the cabin windows, though one of the windows is now free of glass, sealed only with a thin panel of clear ice.

In every direction lie fields of ice, a world of white unmarked by any work of man except this frozen hulk. What fate may have befallen the particular man on the floor of whose cabin I now sleep—the berth is hopelessly small—or the rest of the crew of the *Mary Goode*, I can only guess. There is no clue, or if a clue exists I am too concerned with my own condition and my own fate to look for it or think about it. I can imagine them all bound in by ice aboard this ship, until they chose, over the certainty of starvation, the desperate alternative of committing themselves to the ice.

Patience. Write calmly.

I have lost count of how many timeless days I have been aboard this otherwise forsaken hulk. There is, of course, almost no night here at present. And there are times when my memory is confused. I have written above that it is May, because the daylight is still waxing steadily—and perhaps because I am afraid it is already June, with the beginning of the months of darkness soon to come.

I have triumphed over the white bear. What, then, do I need to fear?

Only the discovery of the truth, perhaps?

I said that I should begin with a description of myself, but now I see that so far I have avoided that unpleasant task. Forward, then. There is a small mirror in this cabin, frost-glued to the wall, but I have not crouched before it. No matter. I know quite well what I should see. A shape manlike but gigantic, an integument unlike that of any other being, animal or human, that I can remember seeing. Neither Asiatic, African, nor European, mine is a yellow skin that, though thick and tough, seems to lack its proper base, revealing in outline the networked veins and nerves and muscles underneath. White teeth, that in another face would be thought beautiful, in mine surrounded by thin blackish lips, are hideous in the sight of men. Hair, straight, black, and luxuriant; a scanty beard.

My physical proportions are in general those of the race of men. My size, alas, is not. Victor Frankenstein, half proud and half horrified at the work of his own hands, has more than once told me that I am eight feet tall. Not that I have ever measured. Certainly this cabin's overhead is much too low for me to stand erect. Nor, I think, has my weight ever been accurately determined—not since I rose from my creator's work table—but it must approximate that of two ordinary men. No human's clothing that I have ever tried has been big enough, nor has any human's chair or bed. Fortunately I still have my own boots, handmade for me at my creator's—I had almost said my master's—order, and I have such furs and wraps, gathered here and there across Europe, as can be wrapped and tied around my body to protect me from the cold.

Sometimes, naked here in the heated cabin, washing myself and my wrappings as best I can in melted snow, I take a closer inventory. What I see forces me to respect my maker's handiwork; his skill, however hideous its product, left no scars, no visible joinings anywhere.

February 1986 • 65550-7 • 320 pp. • $3.50